RUBY
Takes Chicago

Ruby

TAKES CHICAGO

Diann Floyd Boehm

Ruby Takes Chicago

Copyright ©2023 Diann Floyd Boehm

All rights reserved under international copyright conventions. No part of this publication may be reproduced, stored in, or introduced into a retrieval system, or transmitted in any form or by any means, without the prior written permission of the author.

First published in 2023 by

Halifax, NS, Canada
www.ocpublishing.ca

Cover and interior book design by David W. Edelstein

This book is typeset in Dyslexie, a typeface specially designed to be easier to read for people with dyslexia. More information is available at dyslexiefont.com.

ISBN - 978-1-989833-38-4 (Paperback Edition)
ISBN - 978-1-989833-39-1 (eBook Edition)

Ruby Takes Chicago is dedicated to my Grandma Ruby, who shared many of her adventures from the time she was a young woman and gathered the courage to leave her family and friends behind and put her college education to work. The book is also dedicated to my mom, Mabel Adella Harris Floyd, who shared more stories of Grandma's life.

I am blessed to have had these strong women in my life to pave the way to have the strength and determination to pursue my dreams.

CONTENTS

Chapter 1

RUBY ARRIVES

August 1926

The long charcoal-gray passenger train slowed down, blew its whistle, and pulled into the Chicago train station. Ruby sat there for a moment, in shock. She knew she needed to move, but it seemed impossible for her to really be there. Finally, she came out of her stupor, gathered her belongings, put her light-pink cloth hat on, and stepped off the train.

Ruby looked around the giant train station with people hustling to and from their destinations. She took a deep breath in and exhaled.

"Hello, Chicago! I might be from a small town, but get ready; Ruby is here!"

Ruby could already tell this town was very different from home. The temperature, for one, was much cooler. It was August and only seventy-eight degrees. If she were back home, the temperature would have been in the nineties! Ruby looked around, inhaled the smells of Chicago, and once more noticed the large number of people rushing to catch their trains or buy their tickets. People moved so fast, probably because it was a much larger train station, compared to the one in Drumright, Oklahoma, near her hometown of Oilton. Ruby took another deep breath and grinned as she continued taking in her surroundings. She just knew she was ready for whatever this next chapter in her life would bring. She headed for the lobby to look for her dad's friends, Mr. and Mrs. Clark, who had agreed to put Ruby up for a night or two.

"You must be Ruby Dinsmore," said a lady walking up to Ruby with a smile, her hand outstretched.

"Yes, Mrs. Clark?" Ruby asked.

Ruby noted the woman was quite fashionable with her cream-colored, Gatsby cotton cloche hat with a lovely light-yellow flower bloom on top of a knitted bow. Ruby also noted she must be about five foot five, the same height as Ruby since they seemed to meet at eye level.

Mrs. Clark nodded, and they shook hands. "Yes, Sally Clark."

"How did you recognize me?" Ruby asked.

"Your father gave a perfect description of you from head to toe," she said. "And remember, your father and my husband, Tom, are Freemasons; they know how to track people." Mrs. Clark chuckled.

Right about then, her husband walked up, and Mrs. Clark introduced Tom to Ruby. He welcomed her, and they all made their way to their automobile. Mr. Clark placed Ruby's suitcase in the back while Ruby climbed in beside it, and Mrs. Clark joined her husband up front.

Ruby listened to Mr. Clark talk about how great her dad was while Mrs. Clark tried to change the subject and point out sights to Ruby as they drove past them. Ruby had to chuckle. The couple reminded her of her parents, each wanting to discuss a different topic.

Mrs. Clark turned to look at Ruby and smiled. "So, you've noticed that Mr. Clark and I often talk about different things simultaneously. It is just what older married couples do."

Ruby laughed. "It's OK. My parents do the same."

Mrs. Clark gave a sweet glance to her husband, and Ruby settled back in her seat to enjoy the ride.

Not long after, they pulled up to the curb in front of the house. Ruby was surprised there were no driveways like she was used to seeing at home, and the houses were much closer together. She thought they must have their vegetable gardens in the backyard, as there was no room in the front or side yards. Ruby got out of the car, walked across the yard, and approached the beautiful two-story home with a white brick finish. As they entered the house, Ruby found herself in a tiny room that Mrs. Clark explained was designed for boots and coats to be placed before entering the main house.

"What do you do with your winter clothes or muddy shoes when you get home?" Mrs. Clark inquired.

Ruby explained that her momma had a coat closet, and if it snowed or one's clothes got wet, they were left on the front porch.

Mrs. Clark stopped and looked at Ruby with a gentle smile. "Oh." She then tried to

work the lock on the door between the wet
room and the living room.

"Ah, there, I got it. Sometimes the lock
gets stuck, and I have to jiggle it." Mrs.
Clark walked in and welcomed Ruby into
their home.

"Please come in. I'll show you your room
where you can freshen up. Mr. Clark will
bring your suitcase up once he gets the car
parked in the back."

Ruby barely had a chance to notice
anything except a lovely fireplace in the
sitting room to the left as she walked
toward the staircase and followed Mrs. Clark
up the stairs. Mrs. Clark stepped aside and
ushered Ruby into her room and opened the
window for fresh air.

"I hope you'll be comfortable here,"
she said.

"Oh yes, I'm very grateful," Ruby said.
"And I love the room."

Mrs. Clark turned around from opening
a second window, smiled, and motioned for
Ruby to follow her down the hall. Ruby
took in the white wallpaper dotted with tiny
lavender flowers and a tall dresser tucked in
the corner for her clothes before they moved
quickly through the hallway.

"Here is the bathroom with a wonderful

big tub to soak in," Mrs. Clark said as she opened the door at the end of the hall. "Please feel free to take a bath every night—none of this 'only a bath once a week' foolishness. We believe in starting the day off fresh as a whistle! I hear that down south sometimes people don't bathe every day."

Ruby explained it was not the case where she lived, and she appreciated the opportunity to enjoy a bath. Ruby could tell she earned brownie points when she told Mrs. Clark how pretty her claw-foot, porcelain tub was. Mrs. Clark then took out some fresh sheets from the glass linen closet, handed them to Ruby, and told her to make herself at home. She showed Ruby the hooks on the wall to hang the towels to dry once she finished with them.

Mrs. Clark snapped her fingers. "Oh, I almost forgot. There is a long bathrobe for you in the wardrobe in your room. I thought you may not have had room to pack one."

"Oh, that is very kind of you."

"Nonsense, no trouble at all. Now come along."

Ruby put the towel set down on the small freestanding cabinet as they left the room.

Mrs. Clark stopped in front of Ruby's

room, hugged her, and told her how happy
they were to have her stay a couple of
nights with them.

"Now, once you are settled, just come
on downstairs and join me for a cup of tea
before supper. I want to hear all about your
train ride."

"Thank you, Mrs. Clark," Ruby said. "I
would enjoy that."

Once Mrs. Clark had excused herself,
Ruby walked into her room and over to the
window that faced the front yard. "Wow,
I am actually here!" Ruby looked out for
a bit and noted how still it was for a
neighborhood, with no children playing and no
one weeding their garden. It was all quiet. *I
guess they must be inside preparing supper.*

Ruby shrugged and turned and noticed
Mr. Clark must have come up while she
and Mrs. Clark were in the bathroom, as
he had left her suitcase for her. "Great,"
Ruby whispered, and she began to unpack,
pleased to see they had a suitcase rack; not
everyone used them.

Ruby's momma was a stickler about
luggage racks. Ruby recalled how her momma
would lecture anyone who even entertained
the idea of putting a suitcase on top of a
bedspread about how many germs were on

suitcases. And there was no way Ruby's momma would allow luggage on a bed someone would be sleeping in. Ruby smiled, as she could hear her momma's lecture in her head. Ruby picked out a change of clothes and made her way to the bathroom. She looked at the fancy linen closet with all the beautifully pressed linen— sheets folded to perfection with matching pillowcases, and towels pressed and folded as if they were ready to be sold in a store. Mrs. Clark had decorated the shelves with a lace border to enhance the beauty of the linen.

"Oh my, how my momma would love this linen closet," Ruby said under her breath.

Ruby sponged off, as she did not feel comfortable taking a bath just yet. She dried herself, put on fresh clothes, brushed her long auburn hair, and headed downstairs to keep Mrs. Clark from waiting too long.

Mrs. Clark had set out the teacups and had a pot of tea and butter cookies waiting for her on the coffee table in the formal living room. They sat down on the sofa to enjoy the refreshments, and Mrs. Clark began telling Ruby about their home while she poured the tea. She explained to Ruby how she and Mr. Clark had grown tired of how busy the downtown Chicago area was

and wanted to move farther out to get away
from it all. So, they saved and saved, and
this house became available. It had belonged
to a friend who was moving to Ohio, so
they purchased it from them. They had
always loved the home, and now they were
proud property owners. They were living the
American dream.

Ruby told Mrs. Clark she loved their
home. Mrs. Clark smiled at the compliment
and told Ruby that they had lived in the
village of Pennock, close to Logan Square
and Kosciuszko Park, which was close to the
Polish community, and how much she had
enjoyed her neighborhood. She even shared a
little history about the area and its start in
the 1880s. Ruby thought it was interesting
that she felt it necessary to share that
particular information but listened politely.
She could hear the pride in Mrs. Clark's
voice when she shared how they had raised
their children in different parts of Chicago,
but now they had this house and a place
for the two grandchildren when they came
to visit.

As Mrs. Clark spoke, Ruby noted the
living room opened into the dining room.
Ruby assumed the kitchen had to be next
to the dining room. She noticed a Chicago

newspaper and asked if she might read it
later. Mrs. Clark said Mr. Clark had finished
with it, so she certainly could take it to her
room if she was so inclined.

She patted Ruby on the knee. "You'll
have to excuse me, dear, while I check on
supper. You can sit and relax after your long
travel day."

Ruby sat in the formal living room
and looked all around. Feeling a little
uncomfortable in her new surroundings, she
saw a knickknack shelf and wandered over
to have a closer look at the figurines. There
were twelve in all and quite a variety—dogs,
children playing, birds, and kittens.

Time seemed to pass slowly, and
finally after about a half- hour, Mr. Clark
reappeared and greeted Ruby just as Mrs.
Clark called them to the supper table. Ruby
hadn't realized how hungry she was until
her hostess placed the chicken and gravy on
the table. The enticing aroma made Ruby's
stomach growl, which pleased Mrs. Clark
but embarrassed Ruby. They all enjoyed
a meal, and Mr. Clark went on and on
about how much he liked James Dinsmore,
Ruby's father.

Ruby was proud of all the compliments

Mr. Clark had for her dad and was learning to see her dad in a new light.

Mr. and Mrs. Clark told Ruby they enjoyed her company so much and asked her to stay until she found a job. Ruby did not want to take advantage of them, but they insisted. It was a load off Ruby's shoulders, and she told them she would find a way to make it up to them. They continued getting to know each other over supper and then retired to their rooms, as they knew Ruby had had a long trip.

Ruby was so tired she did not even take in the detail of the room. Instead, she just slipped out of her dress, climbed under the covers, and fell fast asleep.

The following day Ruby woke up to the smell of bacon, pancakes, and eggs. After a hearty breakfast, Ruby joined the Clarks at their local church service and met some of their friends. Ruby could tell she would like the church family and appreciated everyone warmly welcoming her.

Later that afternoon, Ruby offered to help Mrs. Clark with dinner. Ruby was pleased to discover that people in Chicago enjoyed the large Sunday meal of the day at noontime, just like in her hometown. Ruby also noted how Mrs. Clark was like her momma; she made sure there were plenty of leftovers for supper so she would not have to cook in the evening. After they ate, Ruby quietly excused herself to comb through the newspaper want ads.

Over supper that evening, Ruby told the Clarks that she had found a few jobs to inquire about first thing Monday morning. Mr. Clark explained how the streetcars worked and which one to take.

"And never refer to a streetcar as a 'trolley,'" he warned. "That's what they call them in New York." He sniffed. "You don't want to be mistaken for a New Yorker here!"

Ruby thanked them for all the information and the map to get around Chicago and headed upstairs to bed. She looked out at the night sky. There were not many stars out, but she took in the surroundings and thought of her momma and wondered what she was doing. Was she OK?

"Oh, how I love my family," Ruby murmured to herself as she gazed out the window at the night sky. She pondered how funny it was that the older she got, the more she missed her momma and her stories. Ruby blew a kiss to the stars, hoping somehow her momma would feel her warmth and love. She turned around and looked at the bed. She could not believe she had a double bed all to herself! A bed so big she and her sisters could share it.

"Oh my!" Ruby sighed and fell back on the bed, smiled, and congratulated herself for all she had accomplished. Then, she folded her hands together, looked up to heaven, and said, "Thanks!"

Ruby always thanked her guardian angel and whoever else might be watching out for her. She knew God had given her extraordinary angels and always wanted to thank them for her good fortune. Ruby picked up the book she had placed on the night table earlier to read before falling asleep— *The Lost Keys of Freemasonry.*

Monday morning dawned, and Ruby had butterflies in her stomach as she dressed in a beautiful blue suit, closed-toe shoes, and simple hat and gloves, ready to find her new job. Mr. Clark did not want Ruby, a single girl, to end up on the wrong streetcar, as there were many that took people to different parts of town. Many people made that mistake and found themselves on the wrong side of town. He had told her the night before but reminded Ruby again how the streetcars operated.

Armed with Mr. Clark's helpful information, she found the right stop, hopped on at the back of the streetcar, paid her fare to the conductor, and took her seat. Ruby took in the sights as the streetcar made its way downtown. Ruby noted that Chicago was more vibrant than Tulsa. She could tell it was a fast-growing city with new people moving there every day. Everywhere she looked, new buildings were going up all over town.

First stop on the list was the Commercial National Bank of Chicago, where they were looking for a secretary. When Ruby arrived at the bank, she was overwhelmed by its size. Huge white columns on either side of the entrance loomed ahead. Ruby stopped and stared at the daunting architecture for a while until someone asked her if she was OK. She shook it off, nodded and smiled, and walked on in. The doors were heavy, and Ruby chuckled to herself, thinking that the outlaws from back home would not even attempt to target this bank. Ruby

smoothed down her skirt and walked up to
the receptionist.

"I'm here about the opening you have for
a secretary." She held up the folded paper
with the job notice circled.

The receptionist shook her head and
informed her they had already filled the
position. Ruby walked out, disappointed but
not discouraged as she crossed off that ad
and looked to the next.

A coffeehouse down the street had an
open manager position, and Ruby thought she
could indeed manage a coffeehouse. As she
walked up to the entrance, she saw a sign in
the window: "Job Filled."

She threw her shoulders back and marched
on to the third place, an easy walk of only
a few blocks. It was an auditor's office, and
Ruby thought that would be right up her
alley. However, Ruby did not even reach
the door before she saw the "Position
Filled" sign.

"Goodness! How long have people known
about these jobs?" she wondered aloud.

Ruby spotted another café and decided
coffee was just what she needed to relax
and regroup, so she headed toward it. Ruby
always felt there was nothing like a good
cup of coffee and a cookie to reenergize a

person. As Ruby settled, she watched an exciting array of people go by. She enjoyed people-watching and would make up stories of where they were going and what they did. Finally, after a cup of coffee, a refill, and a cookie, Ruby took a deep breath, and off she went to a few more places, all located nearby, only to discover others had again beat her to them.

She returned to the Clark home and sat in the living room, rubbing her sore feet.

"I guess finding a job won't happen overnight," she said with a sigh.

"Don't get too discouraged," Mr. Clark said. "It's only been one day." He smiled and gave her the day's newspaper so she could scan the job postings for a new search the next day.

"Go wash up, you two," Mrs. Clark called from the kitchen. "Supper will be ready soon."

When they were all seated at the table, Mr. Clark said grace and then immediately began peppering Ruby with questions about her day.

Mrs. Clark interjected. "Darling, give her time to answer before you launch into the next question." Mrs. Clark gave Ruby a smile, setting her at ease.

"Right," replied Mr. Clark.

Ruby smiled at her well-meaning host. "Well, it was an interesting day. I knew deep down one cannot expect to just come to a new city and find a job on the first day, but I was hoping."

"You are correct," he said. "So, tell us what happened today."

"Well, as you know, I had my list of places to visit, and everywhere I went, the jobs were already taken."

"Oh, that must have been so hard on you." Mrs. Clark clucked her tongue.

"Nonsense!" said Mr. Clark. "This girl is like her dad. She has fire in the gut. I mean, look how she has come all this way."

Ruby had never had anyone tell her she was like her dad, and she took it as a great compliment. "Why, thank you, Mr. Clark." She blushed. "I never thought of myself as having my dad's strength. He certainly never told me."

"Well, don't expect us dads to tell our little girls that. After all, we are just getting used to the thought of girls working outside of the home." He shook his head. "Just remember this, Ruby—if your dad did not believe in you, you would not be here."

"Yes, Mr. Clark, I guess I never thought of it like that."

"Mr. Clark is right, dear," said Mrs. Clark. "Both your parents are very proud of you."

Ruby smiled and thanked them. The rest of the meal was enjoyed with comfortable conversation followed by many compliments to Mrs. Clark.

"Now, Ruby, remember that you have very strong qualifications," Mr. Clark said. "Something is sure to turn up. You just have to be patient."

Ruby thanked him and got up to help Mrs. Clark clear the table. Once everything was in the kitchen, Mrs. Clark told Ruby to go on upstairs for the night and she would finish up the dishes.

Ruby thanked her and retired to her room. As she scanned new job possibilities in the paper, she tried not to let herself become discouraged.

The following day Ruby repeated the process in a different area of the business district, only to have the same disappointing results as the previous day's search. As Ruby prepared for bed, she told herself, "I do not care if I have to mop floors; I have to get a job."

In the morning, the Clarks again told Ruby to be patient, that the right job would come up, and wished her good luck.

"I am not known for my patience," Ruby said. "But I will try to remember your advice."

She thanked them and once more was off on her job search. At the first three companies Ruby had marked with possible openings, the windows all had signs that read "Position Filled" or "No Job Openings."

Undeterred, Ruby thought there would be something at the candy factory, so off she went to see if this would be the place. The candy factory mostly hired women, but at least they paid a minimum wage of 54.8 cents an hour. *That would work*, she thought. Ruby walked in and let the person behind the counter know she was interested in working at the factory. The manager came and took Ruby to his office. She was getting excited, and the interview seemed to be going well— until she heard the dreaded sentence . . .

"You seem like a nice lady," the manager began. "Unfortunately, you're overqualified, *and* we prefer to hire local women."

Ruby said she understood and asked where the nearest coffeehouse was. He told her and then handed her some hard candy to thank her for coming in. Ruby nodded, thanked him, and left.

She walked over to the local diner that the manager of the candy shop had suggested and quietly mulled over the last couple of days. It had never dawned on her that people hired locals over out-of-towners or that a person could be overqualified for a job, so now she was worried. She realized she might have to rethink telling a possible boss about her education to even get her foot in the door. While Ruby sat in the booth, she noticed a customer was about to throw away his newspaper, so Ruby asked him if she might have it.

"Yes, of course." He tipped his hat, handed her the paper, and said, "Good day."

"Thank you, you as well," Ruby replied. Then she remarked to herself, "Well, they may not give me a job, but they have good manners."

While she was poring over the want ads again, scouring the pages for new positions and making notes, another customer came in and sat in the next booth. He cleared his throat a little to get her attention, but Ruby paid him no mind, so he did it louder.

"More coffee, miss?" the waitress asked.

"That would be lovely," Ruby said as she glanced up and smiled.

As the waitress was pouring the coffee, she said in a low voice, "Miss, do not look now, but there's a nice-looking man in the booth across from you trying to get your attention. Don't look!" Then, the waitress said in her normal voice, "Can I get you anything else, miss?"

"Oh no, thank you!" Ruby said as she felt her cheeks getting hot. "I didn't realize he was trying to get my attention," she whispered. She covered her mouth to stifle a girlish giggle.

Ruby paused for a moment and then looked over at the gentleman, who gave her a nod and a smile, so she smiled back and returned to her paper.

"Excuse me for being so forward, but I could not help but watch you pore over the want ads. Are you new in town?"

Ruby looked up, only to see the gentleman had moved to her booth. "You're excused." She pretended to keep reading, then glanced up when he didn't move away. "I do not even know you, so perhaps you could introduce yourself before I answer your questions."

"Oh, pardon me for my rudeness. I am John Wiess, and I work in the area, and this is my coffee hangout when I need a break from the office."

"Office, I see." She laid the paper down, hoping this might be the break she needed. "It is nice to meet you, Mr. Wiess. I am Ruby Dinsmore, new in town and looking for a job."

Mr. Wiess grinned. "I figured as much." He glanced over at the paper. "So, what type of job are you looking for?"

"Well, at the moment, anything that will pay enough for a place to stay, and then later, I'll look for a job based on my skills and qualifications."

"Well, if you are looking for just any old job, maybe I can help. Tell me, can you work a switchboard?" he asked.

"Of course, do you know of something?" Ruby's voice rose hopefully.

"I do, right in the insurance building across the street." He pointed out the window. "So, tell me, Miss Ruby, how soon could you start?"

"Well, it depends; how much do you think they pay?" Ruby asked.

"I know for a fact they pay seventy-five cents an hour, which is much higher than minimum wage, and it is a guaranteed nine-to-five job."

"Seriously? Are you sure?"

"I am quite sure," he said with a smirk. "I know the boss."

"Well, what are you waiting for? Can you take me to meet him?"

Ruby waved at the waitress to get her attention. "We must get there before someone else beats me to the job," she said, just a little breathless. She waved to the waitress once more even though she was already walking toward her. "Check, please!" Ruby said.

Mr. Wiess looked up at the waitress. "Jo, put it on my tab, please."

"Yes, sir!" Jo said.

"Thank you, but you do not have to do that, Mr. Wiess," Ruby said.

"Please call me John." He handed Jo a tip.

Jo looked at Ruby and then back at Mr. Wiess and thanked him, and off she went to the next customer calling her to their table.

"I know I do not have to, but I like to do things I don't have to do. It makes for an interesting day." John stood up. "Now, let's go to the office and let you meet the boss."

John flipped his hat onto his head while Ruby grabbed her purse. They walked out the door together.

"What's the boss like?" Ruby asked, puffing just a little bit as she tried to keep up with John's long stride. "Are you sure he won't mind you introducing me to him unexpectedly?"

"I'm sure it won't be a problem," John assured her. "I know for sure he will like you."

They entered the building and went up to the second floor. John took her over to the switchboard.

"Hello, Liz." He stepped aside to present Ruby. "Please show the new girl how to use the switchboard, explain who is who, and then you may return to your desk. Thank you so much for filling in."

"No problem, sir," Liz said.

"Sir?" Ruby's eyebrows raised about an inch as she looked up at him.

"Yes, Ruby, I am the boss, and you have a job," John Wiess said.

"Oh my, thank you, sir."

"No problem. Learn how to use that crazy switchboard. My office is over there if you need me. I will have you fill out the necessary paperwork at the end of the day."

"Yes, sir," Ruby replied.

Mr. Wiess went into his office, and Liz began the training.

"So hi, I am Liz, as you know. How did you find out about the job?" she asked. "It just became available this morning."

"Seriously? What happened to the operator?" Ruby asked.

"Fired." Liz shrugged. "He gave her many chances, but she was always late to work, leaving the board unattended. The list goes on and on. Today was the final straw when she told Mr. Wiess she needed a week off, as she was 'stressed' from working so hard."

"Oh my, who says that?" Ruby told Liz she had never shied away from hard work unless you counted her attempts to escape plucking chickens back home, but Ruby didn't count that.

"People with rich parents like her do not need a job." Liz paused. "I don't really know why she was working at all."

Liz filled Ruby in between incoming calls, quietly giving her the lowdown on the girls in the office, which made for fun gossip while Ruby learned the names of the men and their office switchboard numbers. Ruby ran her finger down the list as Liz explained who each person was.

Then came Ruby's turn to answer the phone and connect them to the correct office while Liz watched. After about fifteen minutes, Ruby felt she had it. Liz agreed and left Ruby to start her new position.

At first, everything was going smoothly and efficiently. Then, suddenly, the small switchboard lit up like the Fourth of July, everyone calling simultaneously. Ruby started answering and connecting, but after a few minutes, she became flustered and plugged all the wires into the wrong jacks. Then, finally, Mr. Wiess came out of his office and walked straight up to her.

"Ruby, I thought you knew how to work a switchboard?" He stood towering over her with both hands planted on the counter.

Ruby looked up at him for a second as she politely answered the next call and made the connection. Mr. Wiess watched, waiting for her answer.

"If you just give me thirty more minutes, I will be the best operator you ever had," she said in a three-second pause between calls.

"Well, you'd better be," he said with a half smile as he turned on his heel and returned to his office.

Relieved she had won a second chance, Ruby focused on the panel and continued connecting the calls as her brow wrinkled. The day was long and short at the same time. Liz gave her a lunch break, but Ruby ate her sandwich while sitting next to Liz and watching her work. By the end of the day, Ruby was a pro.

"Ruby, can you please stay on a few minutes," Mr. Wiess called from his office. "I'd like to speak to you."

"Yes, of course, sir." The girls exchanged glances as Liz helped Ruby turn the board off and told Ruby she would see her in the morning. Ruby then went and knocked on her new boss's door.

"Come in, Ruby," Mr. Wiess said. "Well, it looks like you got it down. Now can I count on you to be at work on time?"

"Oh, yes, sir," Ruby said.

"Good. Then fill out this application so I can have you on the payroll. You will receive a check every Friday. I hand them out myself in appreciation of your work. I believe in teamwork, and we each have a job to do that makes each of us, and the company, successful. As they say, we are just one part of the whole."

While he was speaking, Ruby finished

filling out the forms. She loved his philosophy and knew she would like working for Mr. Wiess.

"Here you go, sir, thank you," Ruby said as she handed the papers over.

"You are welcome, and welcome to Mutual Insurance."

Before Ruby could thank him, he asked her if she needed a lift home.

"Oh no, sir. You have done more than enough today. It was so kind of you to give me a chance at this job. I will not let you down." Ruby shook his hand, thanked him again, picked up her purse and hat, and went out the door.

Ruby walked out of the insurance building filled with joy; she wanted to pump her fist in the air and scream "Yes!" to the world. Instead, she grinned from ear to ear, and with a skip in her step, she went to the local candy shop she had interviewed with the day before and picked up a box of candy to take to the Clarks to celebrate.

As Ruby walked to the streetcar, she beamed and said hello to everyone she met on her way. Even after she boarded, when new riders found their way to a seat, Ruby smiled and said hello. She received strange looks, and a few men tipped their

hats. When she arrived back at the Clarks'
home, she found Mrs. Clark in the kitchen
preparing supper.

"I can tell by the spark in your eye that
you have good news," she said while drying
her hands on her apron. "Let's go into the
living room, and you can tell me about
your day."

Ruby followed Mrs. Clark, sat down on
their big, overstuffed sofa, and told her the
whole story. Mrs. Clark could not get over
Ruby's strength to accept a job without even
knowing how to do it. They were so involved
in Ruby's storytelling, Mrs. Clark almost
let the potatoes boil over. She quickly ran
into the kitchen and took the pot off the
stove just in time to stop the water from
bubbling over.

"Oh goodness gracious, that was close!"

Ruby followed her into the kitchen, got
out a steel colander, and handed it to Mrs.
Clark to drain the potatoes.

"Ruby, tell me more."

So, Ruby continued where she had left
off—when she connected all the people to
the wrong offices on the switchboard—while
she helped prepare supper. Ruby had finished
her story by the time supper was on the

table, and Mrs. Clark was overjoyed for Ruby and her new job.

Ruby heard Mr. Clark arrive. He always entered the house through the back door. By then, she was not surprised by the entrance to the home, which was unusual to her. As she had learned, there was an automobile alley behind the house where the homeowner could drive to their garage. Mr. Clark had given Ruby a brief history of garages. He explained that she should think of them like a carriage house replacement. The automobile would be safe from the snow, and a garage provided more storage space. He was proud to say that not everyone had a garage, but their neighborhood was forward-thinking in its building plans. Mr. Clark also chuckled when he explained drivers could go down the new streets without parked cars blocking the way.

As Mr. Clark placed his hat and jacket on the rack in the wet room, Mrs. Clark blurted out in excitement, "Ruby has great news for you!"

"Ah, I assume you had a strong interview, my dear?"

"Yes, I did and—"

"Oh, there is so much more to the story,"

Mrs. Clark interrupted. "Hurry, get ready for supper, and Ruby can tell you about it."

"Yes, dear. Hold that thought, Ruby." He winked and made his way upstairs.

The two women set the table, making small talk as they waited for Mr. Clark, who finally joined them. He said grace, and they passed the food around. Once the plates were filled, Ruby told him she had a job, and her first official day was the following day. Mr. Clark was very happy for Ruby.

"Oh, it was how she went about it," Mrs. Clark said. "Dear Ruby, go ahead and tell Mr. Clark what you will be doing."

Ruby proceeded to tell him all about the switchboard job.

"Well done, Ruby! This is truly a new beginning for you." Mr. Clark raised his glass. "Your dad will be very pleased and proud."

"Ruby, tell him how you did not even know how to work a switchboard."

Ruby told the story to Mr. Clark as she had to his wife. He once again told Ruby she was like her dad, who had a "real fire in the gut."

Ruby smiled and thanked him.

"I do think Dad would be proud of me." Then glancing at them both, Ruby said, "Well, I guess when I get my first paycheck, I should look for an apartment or a boarding house for girls and give you back your space."

The air in the room seemed to still as the mood shifted.

"Oh, Ruby," Mrs. Clark began, "I had not thought about the impact of you getting a job. I have enjoyed your company so much." She looked over at her husband.

"After being married as long as we have, over forty years, I know that look," he said. He turned to Ruby. "Ruby, our son and daughter will not be coming to visit for a few months, so why don't you stay here till Thanksgiving? That would set you up with a bit of savings; you will have settled into your job, and you will have plenty of time to find housing."

Ruby looked at both of them, her eyes wide. "Oh, I could not impose. You have already done so much."

"Nonsense," said Mr. Clark. "If we did not want you here, we would be asking when you are moving out."

"Yes, Ruby, you must stay," Mrs. Clark insisted. "You bring so much excitement and energy into our day. The house is alive with you in it. Please say yes."

"Well, if you don't think my dad would mind, it would help me for all the reasons you stated, Mr. Clark."

"Don't you worry about your father; I will let him know it was entirely our idea," Mr. Clark said.

Ruby thanked them. "Well, then you two let me clean up, and you can relax. After all, that is the least I can do."

"That would be lovely, dear," Mrs. Clark said. "Maybe we can catch the *National Barn Dance* on the radio."

Ruby excused herself and let the Clarks enjoy their music. That night, she slept like a baby and awoke refreshed and ready to officially begin her new job.

Chapter 2

A SINGLE WORKING GIRL

SEPTEMBER 1926

Ruby had a spring in her step as she left the streetcar and walked to her new job. Liz was waiting for her at the entrance. They made their way to the insurance offices and proceeded to the employee lounge where Liz showed Ruby her locker. Ruby was then introduced to Mrs. Burk, who gave Ruby her uniform, a blue blazer in just her size. Ruby learned the blazer was to be worn at all times, no matter if she wore a dress, or skirt and blouse. Ruby knew the secretaries did not have to wear them, only the switchboard operators. Next, Ruby joined the other girls as they clocked in and headed to their workstations.

Now that Ruby was part of the team, Liz introduced her to the secretaries on their floor—Helen, Louise, Mabel, and Margaret. The secretaries were very polite and wished her well. Mabel was especially friendly and let Ruby know if she needed anything when Liz was not around to just ask.

Ruby then went to her desk, placed her purse in the lower drawer, and turned on her headset connected to the mini switchboard. Ruby was happy to formally meet the other secretaries, as she had not had a chance to be introduced to them properly the day before.

"Mr. Wiess wanted to be sure you made it through the first day," Liz explained.

Ruby gave a little smile as she scanned the various offices with each secretary sitting outside their boss's door. Ruby thought about how her desk was within walking distance of them, yet she needed to ring their phones to share what line was for them. Oh, the wonders of technology—no more yelling at people to get the phone.

"It's going to be a great day," Ruby whispered to herself. She had written down all the connections and memorized the board the night before. *No more mistakes like yesterday,* she told herself as she took a deep breath. Before she could even let it out, the switchboard lit up and the day began.

As the day progressed, Ruby learned there were breaks every two hours for fifteen minutes; Liz and the other secretaries took turns. The girls received a thirty-minute lunch break, taking turns two at a time. Liz and Ruby were able to share their lunch breaks. Helen and Louise went to lunch together, and Mabel and Margaret were teamed together. The girls were there for each other, or so it seemed. Over the following weeks, Ruby saw the pettiness that would occur in the workplace. There were also affairs that happened on different floors between some secretaries and their bosses; often the wives would discover what was happening, which would lead to an unpleasant scene at work. A couple of the secretaries from other offices had to leave. Ruby was just glad it was not on her floor.

Ruby followed Liz's advice and did not get involved with the girls who liked to party and go out with the men at the office. Ruby enjoyed having a good time, but some

office girls did things that would have never
entered her mind, and besides, she would not
want to disappoint the Clarks.

The Clarks looked forward to Ruby's stories
about her day even when nothing eventful
happened. Ruby left the more salacious
details out. Even so, Ruby found that it
brightened Mrs. Clark's day to hear what
filled a working girl's day.

"You should be happy to be born to the
generation of women working in a man's
world," Mrs. Clark told her.

One evening while Mr. Clark was at a
meeting with his Knights Templar friends,
Ruby and Mrs. Clark were having a quiet
evening in the sitting room.

"If you could go to school, what would
you want to study?" Ruby asked.

Mrs. Clark looked at Ruby, somewhat
puzzled. "I never really thought about it,"
she finally answered. "Us girls knew you
just got married and started a family." She
paused and thought some more. "But, if I
had gone to school, I would have studied
the weather. I am fascinated by the various
cloud formations."

"Oh wow, that is interesting," replied Ruby. "I never thought about studying clouds. If ever I see articles about the weather, I will make sure to share them."

"That is sweet, dear, but now I have Mr. Clark, and we are happy, and there is no reason to think about what could have been." Mrs. Clark smiled and looked at Ruby. "I am content with my life and my family and very proud of the work Tom does for the Chicago Plan Commission. Why, Tom even works with James Simpson and Eugene Taylor, two prominent men who serve on the zoning commission. People do not work directly with these men unless they excel at their jobs. Besides, while he's at work, I have the freedom to enjoy some of my hobbies and social work through the church where I spend time with my friends."

Ruby smiled, reassured that Mrs. Clark was content.

"I understand," Ruby said. "But just in case, reading articles of interest cannot hurt."

Mrs. Clark agreed, and the women continued enjoying each other's company until it was time to retire for the night.

A few uneventful weeks went by, and Ruby was in a routine: wake up, greet the Clarks, and grab a bite to eat. Mrs. Clark always prepared a quick breakfast for Ruby before she left for the office. Ruby had mastered her route to work. She always met Liz at the final stop, and into the office they would go for the day.

Ruby could not have been happier and was very proud of how things were progressing. However, it was sad that women's salaries did not match the men's wages, so they needed to be careful to make ends meet. They didn't have the luxury of spending money on new clothes.

When Liz told Ruby it was high time she got a thicker coat, Ruby explained there was no way she could spend money on a new winter coat. Liz told Ruby about a place she had in mind with great deals and told her to relax. Liz suggested they get together over the weekend, and she would introduce Ruby to the world of thrift shops.

Ruby agreed, and they planned for Liz to fetch her at home at ten o'clock on Saturday morning.

Sure enough, at 10:00 a.m. sharp, Liz knocked on the door, and Mrs. Clark greeted her and showed her inside. Ruby finished tidying her room and came down to join the two women. Ruby assured Mrs. Clark that she would be back in time to help her with supper or any chores.

"Don't worry, dear." Mrs. Clark smiled. "I will have it all taken care of by the time you get back. You run along and enjoy your day off."

The girls smiled, and Ruby hugged Mrs. Clark, who, by this time, she thought of as a second mom.

The girls walked up the road to the streetcars and were on their way. Liz introduced Ruby to Goodwill. Ruby had never been in the store before and was amazed at how many women their age were purchasing secondhand clothes.

"They are just like us, making ends meet," explained Liz. "Buying clothes at Goodwill gives us a chance to dress nicely and still pay the bills. And it helps others by giving them jobs."

Ruby could not get over the quality of clothes people in Chicago donated as she combed through the racks. To her surprise, Ruby found a thick wool coat, a black fur hat, and a pullover sweater. Both girls left with a sack full of clothes, each tickled pink over the deals they found. They did not want to walk around Chicago with their bags of clothes, so they headed to Ruby's place to drop off their purchases.

Mrs. Clark served the girls tea and cookies while they showed off their wares.

"I'm so relieved you found a thicker coat, Ruby," she said. "I wondered how you would handle a Chicago winter with that lighter one you arrived with." She chuckled.

After enjoying the afternoon in each other's company, Liz headed out, as she needed to do some things around her place, including writing letters to family back home. Ruby walked Liz to the door and thanked her once more.

As Ruby closed the door, Mrs. Clark called to her and asked her to come into her bedroom. Ruby found Mrs. Clark sitting on her bed and holding a large box. She asked Ruby to sit down and opened the box to reveal a lovely pair of leather boots.

"Those look brand new," said Ruby.

"They are, in a way, but that is another

story," said Mrs. Clark. "Here, take a look. What size do you wear?"

"A seven and a half, I think," said Ruby as she took the boots that were handed to her.

"I think they might fit even if they are an eight," Mrs. Clark said. "Boot sizes are a bit different."

Ruby tried them on, and sure enough, they fit perfectly.

"Oh, they look very nice, my dear," Mrs. Clark said. "I would like you to have them."

Ruby stuttered, not knowing what to say.

"I am just glad I saved them," said Mrs. Clark. "Now come on, we better get down to the kitchen."

Ruby followed her to the kitchen, and the two women worked together, planning and preparing the supper menu. Mr. Clark was out all day with his friends, and Mrs. Clark wanted to be sure to have a nice Saturday supper ready when he returned.

They fell into a comfortable conversation, and Ruby shared with Mrs. Clark how some things seemed to be the same for everyone, no matter where they lived. She told her how on Saturdays, her momma would do laundry and prepare something for the Sunday dinner to avoid taking too long to prepare a meal after church.

"I do enjoy hearing stories about your momma and life in Oklahoma, Ruby," Mrs. Clark said.

Even though it snowed in Oklahoma, Mrs. Clark knew it was nothing like a Chicago winter. Mrs. Clark explained that despite the weather, she could never leave Chicago. It was home for her and had been all her life, and anywhere else would not seem like home. Ruby said her momma felt the same way. She had her friends and family, and life seemed perfect for her momma just the way it was.

The day came and went, and Ruby prepared for bed, grateful to be ready for the Chicago winter.

Chapter 3

FRIENDSHIPS BLOOM

October 1926

Liz and Ruby met each morning in front of the insurance building, and they would clock in together. Ruby could count on Liz to tell her the ins and outs of the insurance company's employees. Liz was the secretary for Mr. Wiess and George Johnson, his right-hand man. Liz started as a switchboard operator while taking secretarial classes and learning skills like the using the Electromatic typewriter. Liz had worked for the company for two years and had made it a point to know everyone.

Ruby and Liz had something in common, which gave them a special bond. Ruby had assumed Liz was from Chicago, as she knew

so much about the city, but it turned out
she was from Wisconsin, then her family
moved to Detroit, and then on to Chicago.
Even though Liz was not from the South,
she had the Southern disposition, which
Ruby found comforting. She would let Ruby
know when she needed not to take things
so seriously; she used sarcasm, something
Ruby was not accustomed to and found a
bit unsettling.

One weekend Liz shared with Ruby how
her family had wound up in Detroit. Her
dad had read an article that Ford Motor
Company was looking for good men to train
to work the production line. He came home
that very day and told the family they were
moving. He did not even have the job yet,
but somehow, he knew he would get it.

Liz's dad did not care for farming and had
convinced his father that his six brothers
could handle the farm without him. Liz told
Ruby she could hear her grandpa tell her dad
how disappointed he was, but at the same
time, he understood. Her dad even had to
give up his share of the farm he would have
inherited one day. So, in 1913, Liz and her
parents had moved.

"My dad would tell me, 'Liz, we might
have lost the land, but we have something

more substantial—opportunity!'" Liz told
Ruby. "'Never pass up a good opportunity,'
he always said."

It turned out to be an excellent decision
for Liz's family, as her dad excelled and
eventually managed one of the production
lines several years later.

While living in Detroit, Liz decided
she wanted to see the world and told her
parents going to Chicago could be the first
step. At the time, Liz's parents had begun
to understand the importance of a young
lady's education. They wanted Liz to be able
to stand on her own two feet, just in case.
Even if she did get married, she should have
a backup plan in case something happened to
the "breadwinner."

Liz's mom had even taken up midwife
skills, like Ruby's mom, and helped deliver
babies when a woman could not make it to
the hospital.

Over time a mutual trust grew between
the two girls, and even if Liz was with some
of the other girls who loved to gossip, she
just listened and nodded her head in such a
way that the girls were satisfied and kept
on gossiping.

Liz was like an informant for Ruby. Even
though the girls would gossip, they felt

it was OK because they watched out for
each other and did not consider it talking
behind one another's back. It was simply
sharing information.

As time went on, Liz gave Ruby more
insight on Margaret, Mabel, Helen, and
Louise, who had quickly accepted Ruby since
Mr. Wiess had personally hired her. Like Liz,
Margaret grew up in Wisconsin on a dairy
farm. Her parents worked hard, and many
people purchased their milk to make cheese.
Wisconsin was becoming known for its
cheese. Margaret enjoyed books and dreamed
of traveling to England, where her great-
grandparents were from. Ruby saw how she
and Margaret were a lot alike too.

Mabel was born in Pittsburgh,
Pennsylvania, and her dad was transferred to
Chicago when she was about ten. Mabel was
about five foot six and slim. She dressed
modestly and wore beautiful hats. Her curly
black hair went to her shoulders, and even
though the bob was the style of the times,
Mabel had no desire to cut one curl off
her head.

Helen had dark brown hair, cut in the
perfect bob. She was the only one born and
raised in Illinois and was the girl of fashion.
Helen kept up with the latest trends in

everything from clothes to music and dance.
She grew up in southern Illinois but moved to
Chicago after finishing her secretarial course.

One day, Helen and Ruby ended up having
lunch together, and Helen shared with Ruby
how she had dreamed of living in Chicago
because her parents constantly spoke of
the competition between New York City and
Chicago for things such as having the tallest
skyscrapers. Helen once told Ruby she did
not understand what "progressive" meant
when her parents talked about President
Wilson, but it sounded good.

Louise had piercing blue eyes and perfect,
silky, straight blond hair that grazed her
shoulders. She could attract a guy from a
block away. She was the friend to be with
when you went dancing. The guys flocked
to the table to dance with all the girls,
especially Louise. You would think Louise
would be stuck on herself, but quite the
contrary. She had grown up in a reasonably
well-to-do home with her five brothers
in Loveland, Ohio. Louise's older brothers
had protected her from the wolfish boys
that circled. Her brothers would tease her
and tell her she was fat and ugly, so she
believed them. Louise shared with Ruby how
her mother told her not to pay her brothers

any mind, that she was beautiful inside and out. Louise told Ruby that her mom would remind her, "Beauty is one thing, but it is better to be educated than to rely on finding a man to marry and take care of you. Just don't tell your dad I said that."

When she finished high school, Louise attended a secretarial school, and upon completion, her parents encouraged her to move to Chicago to work. They told her she could live in a boarding house for women until she found the man of her dreams. "I am not sure what a man of my dreams would be," Louise told Ruby. "But it is fun to explore the possibilities." Ruby giggled when she recalled Louise telling her that.

One Friday evening after work, Ruby was invited to stay the night with Liz so they could stay out late without any questions asked. Mr. and Mrs. Clark enjoyed knowing all of Ruby's work friends, but Ruby did not want Mr. Clark to tell her dad that she came in late on the weekends.

Helen heard a new local band was coming to the "Blind Pig," which is what they called a speakeasy when they did not want particular ears to know what they were planning. Helen thought it would be fun to see the group. Generally, the Green Mill, also known as the GM, hosted celebrities, and the entrance fee was above their pay grade. The girls heard through the grapevine that mobsters paid the police off to keep the place open. Now and then, the GM would host a band from surrounding areas when there was a break in the schedule for the big names. Unknown bands had an opportunity to perform in front of a crowd, and young people like Ruby and her friends could afford the entrance fee, as they lowered it when up-and-coming bands were playing. When Helen heard about the event for locals, she immediately helped spread the word using the code word "mash," and her friends understood what she was saying.

It was never easy to go to a speakeasy, as they were prohibited, so the girls had to take extra care, especially Ruby, as she did not want to upset the Clarks. Earlier in the week, Ruby would bring one piece of her outfit at a time to work and place it in her locker. Liz would take it to her place, and by Friday, Ruby would have a complete outfit to change into at Liz's before going out for the night. The girls made sure they finished all their work early, and of course, Ruby had it easy, as once the switchboard closed, calls ceased, and she was free to go.

As Ruby prepared for a night of listening to jazz, she decided she was not ready to let the girls in on her love of jazz and her dancing experience. Ruby was still cautious of her new friends and wanted to protect her reputation for any new job that might be waiting for her around the corner. She was already taking a chance by going to the speakeasy, and though she felt it was not the government's business to tell them what they could or could not do, she was a little afraid of what would happen if her boss did find out, not to mention her father.

The girls met behind the Green Mill. The thick metal door of the speakeasy opened, and a huge man looked at the girls, his muscular arms crossed across his chest. "Password," he grunted.

Helen, of course, knew the password. "Tarantula juice," she said.

The doorman waved them in, and a young girl in a tight black dress showed them to their table.

They had worn coats to cover their outfits so as not to draw the attention of any busybodies watching the comings and goings in the area. People always seemed prepared to turn young people—especially young, single girls heading into the forbidden speakeasies—in to the authorities.

The girls had dressed for a night out on the town, and when they took off their coats, Liz remarked how smashing they all looked.

"Good- and bad-looking birds will swoop to our table, hoping to get to dance with one of us," Liz said.

"Oh, Liz, you slay me," Ruby said, and all the girls laughed.

The girls sat down and began chattering about how great the place looked. The other girls had been to the GM, but it was the first time for Ruby, and she took it all in. Ruby could not believe a bar could be so long, and she had never seen smoky mirrors before. The GM had beautiful wooden lights. The stage was set for the band, and the excitement was growing for the music to start and the dancing to begin.

People could choose to sit at bar tables or in booths. One booth was known as the "Al Capone booth," and it always remained

open in case he came to enjoy some jazz
while conducting his meetings.

While all the chattering continued, Helen
called the waiter over and asked to see the
menu for "giggle water." That stopped the
chatter for a moment as the words sank in,
and they realized she was asking for a drink
with alcohol. Just the name made the girls
giggle, and the chattering started back up.

As the music began to play, Ruby recalled
how much she enjoyed dancing and reminded
herself that she had no intention of dancing;
it was not time for the girls to know *that*
part of her past. The few times the girls
had gone out, there had not been any
dancing. All the girls really knew about Ruby
was that she grew up in a small town in
Oklahoma. She knew they assumed she would
not have been exposed to modern music
like "The Charleston" or one of the newer
dances like the Baltimore Buzz. Ruby told
them she would keep her head on straight
and watch out for anything out of the
ordinary that could get them in trouble.

"At least we have one Goody Two-shoes
to watch out for us," Helen teased.

Ruby did not know if that was a
compliment or if it was a relief to Helen that

she was willing to forgo drinking. Ruby just smiled and nodded to all the girls.

Mabel and Helen did not waste any time ordering their favorite drinks, a Bee's Knees and a Gin Rickey. The others were still deciding what they wanted. While waiting for their drinks, they looked around to size up the room. The girls were a little early but did not mind as they watched the crowd build and scoped out the guys as they came in. Helen, the most sophisticated of the bunch, was the only smoker, and she went through a dramatic production as she lit her "smoke," as she liked to call it.

The new local band being featured that night was called The MacDougall Band, and they played all the latest hits. Helen had assured her friends they were good; they could play jazz and some of the new ragtime music. The girls were very happy with the band as they moved to the beat while conversing and watching the crowd grow. The girls were disappointed to see it was mostly couples.

For a while, they thought there would be no single guys, but finally, one group appeared, and then another. The guys scoped out the territory, and before long, Helen and Louise hit the dance floor with some of the

guys who had come in. Ruby and Liz remained
at the table to make sure everyone knew it
was occupied. It was easy to lose a table;
people just came over, sat down, and made
people move, and Ruby would not allow that.
Ruby was known as the "Mrs. Grundy" of
the group because she was a bit prudish and
did not drink. She preferred a fancy beverage
with a cherry on top to give the appearance
of an alcoholic drink.

Liz shook her head as the drinks arrived.
"Why don't you loosen up for once?" she
asked Ruby.

Ruby gave Liz a pensive look. "I like my
head just the way it is," said Ruby. "And
besides, someone needs to keep their senses
if anything happens while we're here."

"Suit yourself," said Liz as she turned
to smile at a smart-looking fellow who came
and asked her to dance.

Off she went to the dance floor while
Ruby remained. A few men did come over,
but Ruby declined and had no problem
smiling, keeping a beat with the palm of her
hands, watching her friends.

The music ended, and the girls returned to
the table to enjoy their drinks.

"Who was that man who came over to the
table?" Helen asked Ruby.

"Just someone who wanted to dance,"
Ruby explained.

"I noticed he did not stay long,"
Helen said.

Ruby nodded. "I told him I just wanted to
enjoy the music and not be bothered by small
talk. He was not pleased when I told him I
was the Mrs. Grundy of the bunch, and he
quickly disappeared."

"Ruby, you didn't!" Mabel said in horror.
She'd heard the tail end of the story when
she sat down to catch her breath.

"Sure I did." Ruby sat up straighter. "I
was not in the mood to be bothered. I got
the heebie-jeebies for some reason when
he walked up. I want nothing to do with
someone who gives me that feeling."

The girls continued chattering about what
gave *them* the heebie-jeebies until Helen
changed the subject.

"That's such a downer!" she said and
ordered another drink.

The girls continued to enjoy the night,
and before they knew it, it was time to
head home.

It was a quiet, chilly night in Chicago, and
they felt something was in the air, so they
chose not to walk and squished into a cab
and split the cost.

When Liz and Ruby arrived at Liz's place, they changed into their nightgowns and immediately crashed into a deep sleep.

The girls slept in till ten in the morning and woke refreshed but ready for coffee. Liz was going on about how much fun the evening was until Ruby interrupted her.

"Oh, my goodness, read this," Ruby said and handed the newspaper to Liz. "Al Capone and his mobsters were spotted outside the Green Mill right before we left, and they caused a ruckus with another mobster and his gang around midnight. The article goes on, but holy smokes! Thank goodness we left early enough to have missed the commotion. We could have lost our jobs had the police gone into the nightclub and found us."

"You are so right, Ruby," said Liz. "I told you there was a weird feeling in the air when we left."

The girls continued drinking their coffee in silence and then agreed it would be a while before they returned to any speakeasy. Their jobs were too important to jeopardize. Ruby left her dance clothes at Liz's, as she didn't

want the Clarks to see her trying to sneak
them in.

When the Clarks returned home from church,
they were pleased to see Ruby was reading
a book in the living room, home from her
sleepover. They invited her to join them for
dinner, but Ruby politely declined, saying she
had had a late breakfast and just wanted to
relax and read her book.

"Did you have a good time, dear?" Mrs.
Clark asked.

"Oh yes, thank you," Ruby said. "Being
with Liz is always fun. I get to learn all
about the gossip from work. Lucky for me
I am too busy at the switchboard to get
caught up and become part of the gossip."

That seemed to be enough for the moment
to quench Mrs. Clark's thirst for hearing
what the young girls of the day were doing
for fun. With that, Ruby went upstairs
before Mrs. Clark could pump her for more
information. Ruby certainly did not want to
tell her the whole story. Ruby's face turned
red when she became nervous, and it was a
dead giveaway that she was hiding something.
Years ago, Ruby had learned to get out of

a room before that happened. She hurried to
her room and plopped down on her bed. She
thanked her lucky stars that she and her
friends had made it home safely.

∽ 59 ∾

TIME FLIES

OCTOBER 1926 (PART 2)

October was flying by! It seemed the weeks since Ruby arrived in Chicago were gone in the blink of an eye, as her mother would say. It was almost her birthday, but Ruby was not telling anyone that it was coming soon. She felt she was a grown-up, a businesswoman, and did not need to make a big deal out of her birthday anymore. Little did Ruby know, Mrs. Clark had a surprise for her, thanks to Ruby's momma.

Mrs. Clark greeted Ruby with a handmade birthday poster and freshly baked banana muffins. Despite herself, Ruby grinned with delight that Mrs. Clark went to all this trouble for her. Mr. Clark had a surprise for Ruby as well. He was going to drive her to work. Ruby was pleased, as the Chicago winds were picking up, and she was beginning to understand why it was called "The Windy City."

With the weather changing, Liz and Ruby agreed not to wait outside the office building for one another. Ruby knew her way around now, so it really wasn't necessary. She entered the building, did her usual change in the locker room, punched in, and went to her desk to prepare for the day. Ruby was glad it was Friday and the end of another workweek.

It was a typical day until break time came around. It seemed all the girls on the floor knew it was her birthday. They each gave her a card during their break. A little birdie had told Liz, and Liz shared the information with the girls. Liz told Ruby to meet the girls at one thirty in the break room while their bosses were out with clients. Doris, one of the secretaries from another floor, would take over the switchboard for fifteen minutes. Ruby smiled and of course knew they were up to something. Ruby entered the break room promptly at one thirty, and her friends called out, "Happy birthday!" Louise had made cookies for everyone, and Helen made a fresh batch of coffee for the girls to enjoy. They chatted a bit and wished her well. Ruby was grinning from ear to ear and shared with them how much it meant to her. She got a little choked up.

The time flew by quickly, and it was time to return to their desks. Ruby relieved Doris, gave her some cookies, and thanked her for giving up some of her break time. Doris, of course, said she was happy to, as everyone took turns helping each other out. Ruby made a mental note and told Doris she would also be delighted to do her part any time she was needed.

When Mr. Wiess saw the cookies on his desk, he stepped out to wish Ruby a happy birthday.

All in all, it was a great day. Of course, the girls wanted to go out and celebrate, but Ruby reminded them she did not party that much, and she wanted to get home, as her parents would be expecting a call and she would not want to let them down.

The girls had grown to respect Ruby and her sensible ways; for the most part, they were not party animals either. They

all enjoyed having a good time but did not
make it a point to go out on the town on a
regular basis. Instead, they preferred to meet
at each other's places or go to the pictures
if a good movie came to town. Plus, some
folks still frowned upon single women going
out unescorted.

That evening Ruby called home, and her
momma was so happy to hear her voice.
Long-distance phone calls were costly,
so they did not stay on for long. Ruby
was pleased to hear the excitement in the
background with her siblings screaming happy
birthday while she and her momma tried to
talk. Ruby shared with her momma about how
her day was filled with surprises. Zola was
pleased that Ruby's friends fussed over her.

Ruby asked to speak to her dad. Her
momma explained that he sent his love, but
he and Will were not in; they had gone on
an errand. Ruby was disappointed that she
did not hear her dad's voice, though she
understood that he had things to do with
her brother. The phone call ended as quickly
as it started, but Ruby found a sense of
comfort knowing her parents were happy.
At least she was able to tell her momma
that she missed her biscuits, gravy, sausage,
and cobbler. Ruby could always picture her

momma smiling her sweet smile whenever
Ruby told her she missed her cooking.

Mr. Clark finished with the evening paper
and offered it to Ruby. She thanked him and
said she would enjoy reading it upstairs and
turning in early. Mr. and Mrs. Clark smiled
and told her how proud her dad was that
she was not going out gallivanting like some
single girls.

Ruby wondered how they knew what her
dad thought but smiled and said, "No, that
is not me. Good night, then."

She walked up the stairs, feeling a little
guilty. However, she did not feel she lied, as
she was truthful, to a point. But she did go
out occasionally, and hopefully, they would
never find out.

Ruby put on a warm flannel nightgown,
got out an extra blanket, kept socks on her
feet, and got into bed, sitting with a pillow
propped up behind her. She opened the paper
and started reading an article about single
women and how society had changed for
the worse. Ruby shook her head. *How is it
even possible people still think this way?*
She thought about her momma's friends, the

courting rituals, and society slowly accepting dating. Ruby knew some things would be different in the big city but discovered she was naive to think the cities would have progressed a little faster. It was a new world for women in the workforce, but companies were not yet ready to offer women paychecks equal to those of men. Nevertheless, Ruby was grateful to the women's movement and how far they had come, and she knew there was more to be done.

She got up, took out her journal, and began writing down her thoughts.

Dear Journal,

Today I turned twenty-two. I am not married; I do not have children; I live far from home. People in my hometown call me an old maid, and even one of my sisters refers to me as a spinster. It hurts, but I am in Chicago, living my dream despite all that. I do not have the perfect job yet, but I am one step closer. I find the big city exciting, but I am shocked at how the general public views a working woman. I read about it every day in the newspaper. I hear comments

on the streetcar as other women
stare at women alone without a man.
Sometimes you can hear men in the
cafés talk about the working girl as
if we are not even there in the booth
next to them.

The men say things like, "The
women are adrift." How could they?
I love men, don't get me wrong, but
why should they be the only ones to
use their brains outside the house?
But dear Journal, I think the men talk
loud on purpose. They want us girls
to hear how they talk about women.
These men complaining about career-
minded women do not even care about
our backgrounds, how we worked just
as hard as them to study to have
a career.

Ruby paused and chewed on the end of
her pencil, then continued.

I had no idea that a city as
progressive as Chicago would still
have people who feel the need for
young women to depend on their
parents or a husband's support. I find
it unacceptable that civic leaders,

politicians, and even the police have
made it known they were alarmed by
this new behavior of working women
going out on a date. Even the term
"date" has a new meaning, and not
one that the older generation approves
of. Courting in public and letting
men pay for movie tickets or buy a
girl drinks or dinner, which is part of
"dating," to them makes a girl look
like a lady of the night! It is absurd.
I even read that some civic leaders
feel this dating scene is a way of
"turning tricks."

Enough of that!

We finally get to vote, and still,
we are expected by society to have
the men hold our hands. To have our
world dictated by the men around
us. Society needs to catch up, as
we women are just as smart as any
man. If my dad can come around and
be proud to have a daughter with a
degree who is able to work in the
business world, then the rest of the
world needs to do the same. Women
adrift! Appalling! We women will show
you who is adrift; you wait and see!

Ruby closed her journal. "Well, I got that out of me. Time to turn out the lights and give thanks for another year. Happy birthday to me!"

Chapter 5

THANKSGIVING

November 1926

One Saturday afternoon, Liz and Ruby discussed Ruby's arrangement with the Clarkes. Ruby knew she had to be moving soon. But where? She had saved enough money but realized that living with the Clarkes protected her from much of the fuss people made about "working women."

Liz had her own apartment, but it still was an all-girls home with women who managed the apartments and kept an eye out to ensure no men went into any of their rooms for any reason. Liz told Ruby how many hardworking girls were assumed to be "easy" by their bosses because they were willing to work outside the home.

Ruby shared with Liz how she used to get upset with her dad for always watching over her, but now she was grateful that he did and had even arranged for her to meet the Clarks.

"It's so unfair that many parts of society still believe a woman should not work outside the home," said Ruby.

"And that the man can be the only provider of the family," Liz said, then sighed.

"I know if I stay here, Mr. Clark, being a Knight Templar who is respected in town, would keep an eye on me like my dad," said Ruby.

The more she fell in love with Chicago, the more Ruby did not mind the Clarks watching out for her. Liz shared how she felt safer in Ruby's company. As much as they both loved Chicago, they had also learned the darker side of the city, where a working girl could get in trouble if caught alone at night. So, Ruby always made sure if she was alone to be home before dark.

Ruby and Liz knew working girls were easy to spot, as they had a similar look— they usually had a bob haircut, smoked, and showed a lot of leg. Ruby had some typical qualities of a working girl, but she didn't have a bob and didn't smoke, which sometimes threw off the people who were waiting for the cigarette to appear.

Ruby enjoyed her afternoon with Liz and loved having a girlfriend she could talk to. She told Liz that once on the streetcar, when she saw an older woman staring at her, she pretended she was looking for cigarettes in her purse and then asked the woman staring at her if she could spare a light. "You should have seen her face!" The two girls chuckled at the story, especially since Ruby detested smoking.

As Ruby got ready to head home, Liz wished her good luck with the Clarks, as Ruby thought she might bring up the topic of her moving out during supper that evening. With Thanksgiving around the corner, Ruby knew she had to move out and did not want to make the Clarks feel uncomfortable about reminding her of the agreement to be out by then, as they were expecting their children to come and visit them.

At the supper table that evening, Ruby braced herself for the discussion.

"Well, Mr. and Mrs. Clark," she began, "I know Thanksgiving is in a few weeks, and so I would love your thoughts on where you think I should look for a place to live. I have been so comfortable here, and I cannot thank you enough for how welcoming you have been."

Mrs. Clark smiled and said, "Well, Ruby, it is funny that you bring it up, as we have some news for you regarding Thanksgiving."

"Oh?" Ruby replied, worried she would have to leave even sooner, but she saw Mrs. Clark give her a smile that generally meant good news.

"Well, we have had news from our children—" Mrs. Clark began.

"And it turns out they have decided to spend time at their in-laws' this year," Mr. Clark said.

"So, you do not have to move out after all," added Mrs. Clark. "That is, unless you want to."

Before Ruby could reply, they asked if she would stay through the holidays either way so they would not be alone.

"I would be thrilled to," Ruby said and sighed with relief. "I simply cannot thank you enough." She got up and hugged them both. "And I would love your input on a proper, well-respected place to live."

They agreed to work with her when the time came, and of course Mr. Clark, not to be condescending but in his polite way,

told her not to worry her pretty little head
about it.

In the past, Ruby would have found the
comment fatherly as intended, but having
read articles about single women working,
it gave her a different slant on the phrase.
However, she politely thanked him, knowing
he had good intentions.

"Ahem," Mrs. Clark said, clearing her
throat. "In fact, Ruby, would you like to
invite your friends who do not have a place
to go for Thanksgiving to come here?"

"Absolutely!" Ruby replied. "None of
my friends on my floor are going home for
Thanksgiving because it is too far. I am sure
they would love it."

"Fabulous!" said Mrs. Clark.

The office closed early on Wednesday,
giving everyone time to make it home. Ruby
spent time helping Mrs. Clark prepare things
so they would still be fresh for the next
day. She shared with Mrs. Clark how she
was never much help with her momma in
the kitchen.

"My momma would be surprised how
well I can cook and bake now. I wish I had

spent more time with her in the kitchen,"
said Ruby. "You know, you mature the older
you get and then realize it was not about
cooking for the family but more about special
moments with your momma that you can
never get back." Ruby shook her head and
sighed. "When I think of moments like that,
Mrs. Clark, I get a little teary-eyed because
I have the best mom in the world. I hope one
day I can make it up to her."

Mrs. Clark came over and hugged Ruby.
"You already have, my dear," she said. "You
are living the life you dreamed of, and she is
so proud of who you are becoming. She told
me so." She gave Ruby an extra squeeze.
"Now then, let's make some brownies and
pumpkin pies. I have a wonderful recipe you
can share with her one day."

Ruby smiled and nodded.

Ruby woke up to the smell of turkey already
in the oven. *You know it is Thanksgiving Day
when you wake up to the aroma of the big
bird cooking*, she thought. Ruby could tell
Mrs. Clark was excited to have a new crop
of people to cook for, but she finally gave in
to Ruby's friends' requests to let them bring

something. Mrs. Clark made a list, and the girls selected what they would make from the list. She also let her friend Mrs. Thomas contribute to the meal. Mrs. Clark agreed it would lighten her load, but she would do the turkey, dressing, gravy, biscuits with butter, and pumpkin and mince pies. Mrs. Clark wanted a grand harvest celebration and a feast for all their guests.

Liz arrived early to help greet guests and took care of bringing their coats and other winter belongings to the wet room. As each one entered the home, dressed in their Sunday best, they referenced the weather, incredibly grateful that the snow had stopped and the temperature was to be a high of forty degrees. Mrs. Clark joined in the small talk about the weather as she welcomed everyone, while Ruby took the food they had all brought into the kitchen.

Helen brought flowers for the centerpiece, Liz brought green bean casserole, and Louise brought sweet potato casserole. Mabel made her mom's favorite baked sweet potatoes with marshmallows, and Margaret brought mashed potatoes.

Mrs. Clark enjoyed getting out her fine china and crystal and setting the dinner table. She had a large dining room table with

two leaves, and they had added two extra
chairs to accommodate everyone.

Once everyone was seated, Ruby smiled
across the table, enjoying her new friends
and the Clarks on a frosty Thanksgiving
Day. The Clarks had invited Mr. and Mrs.
Thomas, a couple from the church whose
children could not make it home. In addition,
their dear friend Hubert Belcher and his
son James, who had both lost their wives
that year to pneumonia. It was a grand
Thanksgiving feast. Mrs. Thomas brought
what she called her "old-fashioned chicken
soup," which was her mom's recipe, and
cranberry relish.

Mr. Clark officially thanked everyone for
joining them and gave the blessing. After
the official "Amen," Mrs. Clark had James
begin by serving himself, and the passing
of the food began. Great excitement and
conversation started as the food was passed,
and Mr. Clark began to carve the turkey. At
first, the conversation was about how the
food tasted, and polite compliments were
given to each person who brought a dish.
Then the conversations moved into more
personal discussions. Ruby noticed James
and Helen sharing some moments of private

small talk and wondered if anything would blossom from it.

Most importantly, everyone joined in the conversation as topics came and went in a natural flow. There were no awkward moments, as politics was never to be discussed at the dinner table. It was a meal to be enjoyed by all.

Ruby knew she had much to be thankful for as she looked around the room and saw everyone enjoying the meal and camaraderie. For a moment, she thought about her parents and family but realized she needed to stay focused and be present, to avoid being impolite.

Ruby's friends helped clear the table so that Mrs. Clark could relax with her friends. Louise filled the large farmhouse sink with sudsy water, and Helen and Mabel scraped the plates clean and handed them to Louise to soak. Ruby put on the water for tea and coffee. Then the girls brought out the various desserts and the dessert plates and bowls.

Comments ranged from "Oh, I could not eat another bite, but I will" to "Oh my goodness, I will have a little of everything," which pleased Mrs. Clark.

Over dessert, the Macy's Christmas

Parade in New York City was the topic of conversation, as there had been an extensive article about it in the newspaper. It was the third year for the parade. James told the group how he and his wife had seen the first one in New York, and it was incredible—the balloons, the parades, and the crowds of people. When Santa appeared, the crowd went crazy with excitement. The joy on children's faces was a sight to behold. They all agreed that one day, they would see it in person.

When everyone finished their dessert, they adjourned into the formal living room and continued to have a lovely time conversing. By the night's end, everyone was in a joyful mood and excited for the holiday season. The Clarks enjoyed getting to know Ruby's work friends even better, and as Ruby's friends said good night, Mrs. Clark told them they were always welcome to come and visit.

Ruby was pleased with how the evening had turned out. She showed her friends to the door. Mabel had a car and drove all the girls home. Ruby thanked Mr. and Mrs. Clark for a magnificent Thanksgiving and said her good-nights. Ruby thought of her family as she got ready for bed. She missed them and wondered how their Thanksgiving had been.

It was too expensive to call home, so Ruby
sat down and wrote a letter, which made her
Thanksgiving complete. As she fell asleep,
she thought about how lucky she was and
how things were working out.

Ruby spent the rest of the Thanksgiving
weekend helping Mrs. Clark get her kitchen
and china cabinet in order. The following
week was uneventful, as Ruby had mastered
her job and worked her way into being a
valued member of the team. As she turned
off the switchboard one evening, Mr. Wiess
called her to come into his office. Ruby
could not imagine what he was going to say,
and it was making her nervous. Nevertheless,
she knocked on his door.

"Ruby, come in and take a seat," Mr.
Wiess said as he looked up from his desk.

Ruby smiled and quietly sat down in front
of his desk. She waited for him to speak.

"Yes, ah, Ruby, it has been several
months now you have worked with us, and I
wanted to know how you like your job."

"Oh, just fine, sir," she answered, leaning
forward. "I appreciate you giving me a chance
to work here."

"Well, that is good." He took off his glasses and leaned back in his chair. "Now, if my memory serves me right, you had told me you wanted a job to get some experience, and then you would look for another one based on your new skills. Is that right?"

Ruby twisted her gloves in her hands. "Yes, but I would not have told you had I known you would be my boss."

"Don't worry, everything is fine, Ruby. There's no need to be nervous, but I do admit that I'm a trifle worried."

"Oh?"

"Ruby, you are a good employee, and it dawned on me I do not want to lose you, but I know you will start looking for a different job soon, if you haven't already." He raised his eyebrows and kept a steady gaze as if trying to read her body language, but she sat perfectly still. Ruby's dad had taught her to always keep a poker face.

"I know that you went to a top business school, Chillicothe," Mr. Wiess continued, "and I thought you could tell me exactly what it is you learned to do in business."

"Well, sir, first of all, I have not begun looking for a new job, as I had not planned to look so soon. And I'm quite enjoying working here." Ruby paused. "Regarding my

particular skill, well, it is in accounting. But
unfortunately, I did not get a chance to do
any internships. Still, I did learn how to be
a quality bookkeeper, and I took classes on
how to manage an accounting department so
that I could work for a larger corporation."
She threw her shoulders back and folded her
hands on her lap.

"Well, Ruby, I felt you had some other
skills we could use here. How would you
like to work in our accounting department?"
He put his hand up before Ruby could
speak. "Before you answer, let me tell you
about it."

"Excuse me, sir, if you do not mind, may I
tell you what I know?"

He smiled. "You may."

"Well, the accounting department is
one floor down, in room 319, and consists
of three accountants in charge of various
divisions of the insurance company, and
you have one manager, Mr. White. It is
easy for me to know that as the operator,
but I also looked into the accountant
job responsibilities." She looked at him
and waited.

"Ruby, you're right!" He slapped the
desk. "And, truth be known, I already knew
what you studied and your grades from the

business school. But I just wanted to give you a chance to tell me, as you didn't really have the opportunity to talk about your abilities in a formal interview here."

"Oh, well, thank you, sir."

"You are welcome. Now I have good reasons for asking these questions, and the main one is that I am acquiring a small insurance company, and it is in my best interest not to overwork my existing accountants but to add another one."

Ruby tried to keep her best poker face, wanting to keep the upper hand in this situation, but the butterflies in her tummy were winning.

"Ruby, I would like you to work two more weeks in your current position and then move to the accounting department. This gives me time to interview for a new operator, have you train her, and then move you over to accounting. You will work with the men there, and they will bring you up to speed. Then when the smaller firm joins the company, you will be responsible for that section. As you know, Mr. White is the supervisor and oversees everyone's work." He paused. "So, what do you think?"

"Sir, I take it this is an interview for a new position, correct?" she asked.

"That is correct, but an informal interview since you are already working here."

"Well, I would like to make it formal so that I may feel comfortable asking some basic questions." Ruby took out a notepad and pencil from her purse.

"Fine, Ruby. It is a formal interview. What would you like to know?"

"Well, to begin with, I have not had much time to think about this, and I am delighted for the opportunity, but there are some issues I need to address."

"OK."

"Well, first, what would the salary be? Then, what are the overtime benefits, especially during tax season? Finally, do the same holidays apply as well as vacation days?"

"Well, Ruby, you do jump right to the heart of things." He clasped his hands as he placed his elbows on the desk and leaned in to answer her questions. "Salary . . . you will be happy to know your salary jumps to sixty dollars a week. Yes, you do have overtime, and you get paid an extra seventy-five cents for every overtime hour you have to work during tax season, but note that your job is to make sure you do not have to do much overtime. In addition, you receive a week off with pay for vacation, and you rotate with the other accountants. They have a system that Mr. White will share with you. Do you have any other concerns?"

"I do," she began as she finished writing down what he had told her. "All the accountants are men. How will they feel about having a woman working with them? I do not want to be a secretary and make their coffee. I expect to be treated with the same respect as the men. I assume the salary you are offering me is equal to their pay?" She smiled as one eyebrow rose with her question.

"Ruby, if you do not beat all. Most employees would have said yes, walked out of here, and been happy. However, after watching you over the past months, I know that you can handle the men in accounting. The truth is, I had the accounting manager watch you from my office on several occasions. Only three days after you began working here I could see what your skills were, and from that point on, we've been grooming you for the new position. You see, Ruby, several things are going on here. Besides growing my company, I want to be an example of how to manage a cohesive work environment. Second, I want to have women

working in various departments. If you notice,
I have men and women working as agents,
and by now, you have come to be friends
with several of them. You get along with
people, and if you do not mind me saying,
they enjoy it when you bring in some of your
homemade treats." He grinned, lightening the
mood a bit.

"Thank you, sir. So do you think I will get
along with the men as their colleague, not
just the lady who brings treats?"

"Excellent question. As I shared with you,
Mr. White knows I've been wanting to hire a
woman and has already observed you while he
and I worked on some accounting issues. He
watched how your personality won over the
staff, both the men and women. He likes the
idea that you are familiar with the company,
instead of hiring someone off the street. He
finally told me today that he agrees with
me that you should move over and begin
training in two weeks, to smooth such a big
transition from managing the switchboard to
an accounting role. He felt your personality
and professionalism would be a perfect fit
for his department. He told me that when
he met you at a company function and asked
you about your family back home, you spoke

about all your brothers. He knew then that you are quite capable of handling yourself."

"Oh, who knew having all those boys around me growing up would come in handy," she said and stifled a giggle. "I have two more questions: one, you still have not answered the question about equal pay." Ruby looked at him and did not flinch.

He was quiet. To Ruby it felt like an eternity, but she sat still. Finally, Mr. Wiess spoke.

"Well, Ruby, to be frank, I know that women should be paid the same as a man for the same work," he began, "and for the most part, I agree with that new way of thinking." He paused. "But, as you noted, it is all men in accounting, and they all have families. I spoke with Mr. White, and we agreed on your salary. It is ten dollars less than the men, but they have been working for me for several years, and you are just starting. As I said, I am offering you sixty dollars a week, but if you do well and have a good review after four weeks, we will raise you to sixty-five dollars a week. You have benefits, and you get a paid vacation, like the men. I hope you will find that more than reasonable. What is the second question?"

"Well, it is a bit more on a personal
level, if that would be all right?"

"Of course, go ahead." Mr. Wiess leaned
back in his chair.

"Well, sir, all the men are married, which
makes it easier to say yes, but it will be
important to me that the wives do not see
me as a threat. I come from a small town,
and sometimes the women let their minds
go to the gutter, and I do not want to be a
source of their worry. I already had to assure
some of the women here that you did not
know me when I was hired, and they were
watching like hawks to see if you would ask
me out."

"They were?"

"Yes," replied Ruby. "And I was glad you
did not ask me out, but then I also could
not help but wonder what was wrong with me
because, at first, when you sat down at the
booth, I thought you found me attractive.
I am not suggesting anything; I am just
saying I am so glad I can honestly say
there's nothing between us. I want to be a
professional woman and open doors for other
young girls to be businesswomen." Ruby
sighed and shook her head. "Did you know
every time you have me stay after hours to
work, some of the girls start gossiping about

it? I heard through the grapevine that two women went across the street for coffee one evening and waited to see if we would come out of the building and act inappropriately. I had to stop that talk when they finally asked me how I hid our relationship so well. It annoyed me so much to know they were spying on me. For heaven's sake, you would think they were one of the Freemasons. So, I gave them a piece of my mind, and from that day forward, they respected me, and we became friends. We've even gotten together on the odd weekend." She paused to see how her boss was taking this information, smoothed her skirt, and took a deep breath before continuing. "I tell you, sir, girls can be mean to one another in the workplace."

"So, tell me, Ruby, they told you they go across the street for coffee and spy on people from the workplace?" he asked.

"Yes, I would not make that up. That is between us, sir, but you watch. They are now wondering why we have been in here for so long, and frankly, I do not want to be thought of as one of those girls who are working just to catch a man. I work because I am smart enough to have a professional job and, maybe one day, when the time is right, be a wife and mother."

He shook his head. "Of course, of course, no problem. Now about the job, do you want it?"

"Absolutely! The sooner, the better," Ruby said. "I will make the sign for a new operator for the window myself!"

"Not so fast, Ruby. I want to tell staff at the right time, so all of this is between us, for now. You can just tell the gossip girls that you had to fill out paperwork about your past employment for the office. Now, do you want to have some fun with them?"

"Depends on what you have in mind."

"Well, first, let me backtrack and share with you that when I first saw you, I thought you were beautiful, but in reality, I did come over to you because I needed to hire someone as soon as possible. I also want you to know I have never asked out any woman who has worked for me, as I do not want a nightmare at the office if things go wrong. I keep my private life private. Understood?"

"Clearly," Ruby said, satisfied with his answer.

"Now for some fun. Let's walk out of here and smile at one another as we walk over for a coffee and run into the girls waiting to 'catch' us. What do you say?"

"As long as we never let them know I told you they were there."

"Deal." They shook hands and then gathered their things and walked out.

As they crossed the street, they knew the girls were most likely watching them, so they hammed it up. However, Ruby took care not to walk too close to Mr. Wiess as they entered the restaurant.

When they walked in, Jo seated them just two booths away from Louise, Margaret, Mabel, Liz, and Helen.

"Thank you, Jo." Mr. Wiess motioned for Ruby to sit.

Ruby sat and stifled a giggle, as she could see the girls squirming and slinking lower in their booth. Ruby knew the girls could hear them as the little charade continued.

"Ruby," Mr. Wiess said, "thank you for joining me for some coffee. Would you care for a bite to eat?" He slid the menu over to Ruby.

"Oh no, thank you, Mr. Wiess, just a coffee, thanks. I need to get home to dinner."

"Well, I kept you late filling out all that paperwork, so the least I can do is buy you a light snack before you go home."

"OK, if you insist."

"I do insist." He perused the menu. "Let's have dessert, and you can worry about dinner later."

Ruby thought, *Gosh, now I wish I had a different job. I could fall for this guy.* For a brief moment, she felt her face turn crimson and thought for sure he could tell what she was thinking. He gave her one of his charming smiles.

Jo came to the table and asked, "Are you ready to order?"

Ruby could see the girls two booths down straining to hear the conversation between her and Mr. Wiess. She smiled, knowing the plan was working.

As Ruby and her boss shared a giant piece of chocolate cake and coffee, he asked her about her family and life in Oklahoma. Ruby talked nonstop about her family and realized she had monopolized the conversation. Mr. Wiess did not appear to mind, as he seemed genuinely interested.

Finally, Ruby told him she needed to get home.

Mr. Wiess understood, gave her a wink. "Look, Ruby, when we are on our own, please call me John. After all, I call you by your first name."

Ruby squinted at him and whispered, "I'm
afraid that would not be proper. I might
get in the habit and slip up at work." She
grabbed her purse and gloves on the bench
beside her. "Now I need to go."

"Well, thank you for joining me. I did need
a pick-me-up after such a long day," Mr.
Wiess said. "I appreciate you telling me a
little bit about Oklahoma, as I will be going
to Tulsa soon for a business meeting. Since I
kept you so long, how about my driver and I
give you a lift home?"

Ruby heard Liz gasp and saw her clamp
her hand over her mouth.

"Please excuse me. I'll be right back."
Mr. Wiess stood up and went to the
men's room.

As he walked by the girls' booth, they
squeezed together and sank even lower under
the table.

When Mr. Wiess returned from the men's
room, he tripped over one of the girls' feet.

"Oh," he said and caught himself on the
back of the booth.

"Oh no!" Ruby jumped up, thinking a
catastrophe was about to happen.

"Oh no," said Louise from under
the table.

"Oh no," said Jo.

"Is there a parrot in this place or is there an echo?" Mr. Wiess looked to see what he had tripped over and saw the girls hunkered down in the booth.

"Oh, hello, girls." He smirked at his clerical staff. "Is there something you're hiding from?"

"Oh, we were all looking for Louise's key," said Liz. "She's dropped it, clumsy girl."

"Yes, she dropped her key, but we have not been able to find it," agreed Mabel.

Louise turned her back and fumbled in her purse. "Oh, look, I have it now."

"Great, great," the others said in a chorus of tut-tuts, their limbs tangling as they sat up straighter in the booth.

"Glad you found your key, Louise," Mr. Wiess said. "Would you girls care to join Ruby and me? Jo, could you kindly bring some menus, please?"

"Oh, sir, that is OK—" Liz began.

"No, no, I insist." Mr. Wiess waved away her weak protest. "I haven't taken the team out in a while. Ruby had to stay longer to fill out forms, and I made her come here, but I assume you all heard everything anyway."

"Oh no, we were looking for a key the whole time," Liz said.

The girls nodded their heads in agreement.

"Fine, then. Let's all move over to a bigger table, my treat!" He turned to the waitress. "Jo, hamburgers for everyone and fries; after all, it is the weekend."

"Do you want them with the works?" Jo asked.

Mr. Wiess nodded yes.

Ruby was stuffed after the cake but found she had no choice but to accept. Hopefully the Clarks wouldn't delay supper for her.

They all enjoyed their time, and Mr. Wiess told them how much he appreciated their work.

"No more work talk; let's just enjoy the meal!" he proclaimed.

They all smiled, laughed a bit nervously, and started eating. Everyone looked at each other as if to say "What do we talk about now?"

Ruby broke the uncomfortable silence. "Well, besides eating these delicious and decadent fries, let's take this opportunity to get to know one another. How about everyone shares one of their favorite things they like to eat that their momma makes?"

The girls were supposed to be this new generation of modern women, but there was still a bit of innocence and charm in the table talk about life in general.

Ruby said, "You go first, Liz, and then you pick someone to go next!"

"OK, let's see, my mom makes so many things! I love her baked chicken. Your turn, Helen."

Helen laughed. "Oh, that's easy. My mom makes the best beef stew ever! I cannot get enough of it during the wintertime. Louise, your turn."

"I love my mom's lasagna. Mabel, your turn."

"My mom makes a deliciously moist meatloaf with brown gravy. She makes it every time I go home. Mr. Wiess, now it's your turn."

"Ladies, you are certainly making me homesick." He sat back, looked up, and smiled. "My mom died a long time ago, but I remember her letting me lick the spoon of the chocolate cake bowl. So, eating chocolate cake is my favorite thing."

"Aw, that is so sweet," the girls said in unison.

Mr. Wiess looked at them and cleared his throat. "Yes, right, Ruby, you started this, so your turn now," he said, lightening the mood.

"Well, my mom is the best cook in all of Oilton as far as I am concerned, but if I had to choose something, I would say her biscuits!"

"Yummy, I love biscuits!" Louise said. "Say, I have an idea. One Friday night, let's all get together, and everyone brings their favorite dish."

"That's a good idea, but why don't we do it on a Saturday, so we have plenty of time to cook," suggested Liz.

"I like that idea as well. Why don't we ask the whole office, and then everyone can bring something, and we can have an old-fashioned potluck supper? I am sure the others on our floor would love to join in," Ruby added.

"A what?" Liz asked.

"Well, at home, we call it a 'potluck supper.' Everyone brings something, but you have no idea what they are bringing," Ruby said with a big smile.

"Well, what if you bring something nobody likes or it's all meat and no dessert?" asked Liz.

"Trust me, there are always plenty of desserts! I could see if the Clarks would like to host the first one and get back to you on Monday."

Mr. Wiess spoke up. "Ladies, if I am invited to this potluck, I would like to suggest we have it at my home. I have plenty of room. But for sure it would have to be next Saturday, as after that everyone is thinking of the holidays."

"That's very kind of you, Mr. Wiess," said Liz. "Thank you so much. We all will play a role, but Ruby and I will map it out. We can work on it on Monday during our breaks."

Everyone agreed.

Mr. Wiess paid the bill and told the girls he would give them a ride, but it would be a tight fit. Mabel, Helen, and Louise declined the offer, as they had other plans. Margaret, Liz, and Ruby accepted, and they all hopped in the back of his car. Mr. Wiess explained to the driver what was happening and said to come back and pick him up after taking the girls home. The girls talked and laughed nonstop. Ruby noticed several times the driver glancing at them in the rearview mirror. Liz was the last stop before Ruby, and Liz wanted to use this time to talk about the charade. Ruby did not want to have the conversation, so she distracted Liz by asking the driver to tell them about the town's history.

Liz shook her head but didn't push it. They pulled up to her place, and as she got out, she said to Ruby, "You *will* fill me in soon!" Ruby nodded, and off the driver went.

On the drive home, Ruby told the driver how she felt so lucky to be in Chicago. He just smiled and let Ruby talk. When the driver pulled up to the Clarks' home, she thanked him and got out.

Ruby entered the house, gave Mrs. Clark a big hug, and asked if she could call her parents to share some good news.

"Of course," Mrs. Clark said.

"Thank you," said Ruby. "And you're welcome to listen in. It's very exciting."

Ruby rang her parents, and her momma answered. Ruby smiled at Mrs. Clark as she began to tell her momma all about the upcoming promotion. Mrs. Clark gave a quiet clap to Ruby as she smiled with delight. "Thank you," Ruby mouthed to Mrs. Clark.

Zola was thrilled for Ruby. "I can't wait to share the news with your father," she said. "Ruby, you truly are a professional businesswoman! I miss you so much, but you are living your dream. I'm proud of you. I know your dad will be too."

After Mrs. Clark heard the news, she stepped away to give Ruby some privacy. Ruby could see that Mrs. Clark was happy for her but knew she was also a bit sad that her guest would be moving on at some point.

Ruby hung up the phone and entered the kitchen.

"Congratulations, Ruby." Mrs. Clark hugged her. "We will have to celebrate when it is official. But first, you must tell Mr. Clark and me all about it over supper. How did it happen? What did your boss say?"

"Oh, Mrs. Clark," Ruby began, "it was such a day! I'm afraid I don't have any room for supper, as Mr. Wiess treated me and the girls to a meal." She saw the surprise on her face and quickly continued. "But I will keep you company and tell you the whole story."

They all sat at the table, and the Clarks listened, periodically interjecting with some of their own adventures from their younger days. When it was time to turn in, Ruby did not read a book, as usual; she was too excited, so she wrote in her journal and then a few letters to her college friends. She wanted to catch them up on her news and find out how things were with them. It was relaxing to write, and **Ruby** retired for the night after preparing the envelopes to take to the post office in the morning. *I mustn't forget to drop these off before work.* **With** that final thought, **Ruby** closed her eyes and listened to a frigid wind howling through the trees outside.

Chapter 6

SECRETS REVEALED

DECEMBER 1926

The staff meetings took place in the main lobby on the ground floor, and the secretaries were shocked when Mr. Wiess announced the changes being made to the office staff. Ruby could feel the coldness in the room as the girls congratulated her in the presence of their boss. Ruby felt a chill run down her spine as she noticed none of the women were conversing while waiting for the elevator; of course, that was not like them. They were constantly chattering with each other. Ruby decided she would take the staircase to give them time to talk about what had transpired before they returned to their desks.

The secretaries had different break times, and Ruby knew she was the gossip of the day. Her friends were happy for her, but Helen had the guts to ask Ruby if she had to do anything special to move to the accounting department.

"It's always been a floor of men only," Helen reminded Ruby.

Ruby was shocked that Helen asked the question so all the girls could hear.

"We are all just puzzled," Helen continued. "Have you been pretending to be all innocent, and in reality, you are one of those 'charity girls'?"

Ruby was insulted that Helen would think she was one of those girls who went on dates for a free meal and movie and would then "put out." "Helen, I thought you were my friend," she said. "Seriously, how could you even think, much less say that? I have been nothing but professional with Mr. Wiess and every other man here." She crossed her arms and glared at Helen and the other girls listening in. "I am worthy of being in that office, and Mr. Wiess knew I would be looking for a job in accounting when he hired me." She let out a frustrated huff. "It just so happens that he has an opening and wants to be the first in the insurance industry to have a woman in accounting. I thought you would be pleased."

Ruby started to walk away and turned back. "I have a degree from Chillicothe College in Missouri, you should remember me telling you." She sighed. "Honestly, Helen, I'm hurt." She turned to the rest of the girls, her voice rising an octave. "And I'm shocked that you wouldn't be more supportive of me helping to break the stereotype."

Mr. Wiess walked out, and all the girls returned to their desks except for Helen, who excused herself to finish her break.

He walked over to Ruby. "Are you all right?" he asked.

The girls looked up to see what she would say. Ruby looked at them and raised an eyebrow. "Oh yes, you know us girls, we are always planning. Helen was sharing some thoughts with me. You know, the potluck is in a few days."

That seemed to satisfy her boss, and he told her he had put a want ad in the paper for a switchboard operator and hoped he would get some responses soon so she could start training her replacement.

Later that afternoon, Helen saw Ruby in the locker room and walked over to apologize. Ruby was very cold and distant but accepted her apology, then shut her locker and walked out. Liz caught up with Ruby, told her to blow it off, and explained Helen's frustration with her job.

"You probably didn't know, but Helen wants to move up the ladder herself," Liz told her. "But there really is no way to move any higher, as she doesn't have the education you do."

Liz went on to tell Ruby that receiving a promotion so soon generally does not happen without strings attached. Even though Ruby had addressed the issue right away, there was still a chill in the air. Most of the women remained aloof toward her. After work, Liz and Ruby went to the café and continued their conversation over hot chocolate. Ruby shared with Liz how she had dreamed of being a professional businesswoman when she was young and how the women's movement had inspired her to use her mind and enter the workforce. Ruby could tell Liz was listening intently, so she shared how she had decided to continue her education, so if she ever had to make it on her own, she could. Liz leaned in as Ruby spoke honestly about her dreams.

"It never entered my mind that other professional women would be cruel to someone trying to make it in a man's world," said Ruby. "I can understand my sisters, mom, and friends back home. They've never been out of Oilton. Well, I take that back; they have been to Tulsa, which is just up the road, and a few other towns close by. But this reaction from Helen, and society in general, should not be tolerated in the workforce."

Ruby looked Liz straight in the eye, her fiery attitude spiking, and continued. "People should really move on, get rid of their outdated thoughts, and quit throwing stones . . . especially women against women! It's just not fair!"

Liz sighed. "I guess life is not meant to be fair," she said. "You just live it and make the most out of the cards you are dealt and the decisions you make."

Ruby shrugged. "Wow. You sound like my momma." She grinned.

"I did sound a little profound, didn't I?" Liz laughed.

The girls smiled at one another and sipped their hot chocolate.

Finally, Liz looked at Ruby with knitted eyebrows.

"What?" asked Ruby. She paused, then asked again. "What?"

Liz pursed her lips. Then she said, "I want to tell you something, but it is so big that you must promise to keep it to yourself. Do you promise?"

"Sure, I promise," Ruby replied.

Liz narrowed her eyes.

"I promise!" Ruby said again.

"Well, it is big. I mean over-the-top big."

"OK, go on. I said I promise."

"OK, remember how I told you about a childhood friend named Doug? His granddad has a farm in Wisconsin . . ." Liz began.

"Yes, I remember," Ruby said. "And?"

"And, well, remember me telling you that his dad decided to move to Detroit like my dad and work for Ford?"

"OK . . . and?"

"Remember when I could not go with you one weekend to shop for boots at the thrift shops?"

"Yes . . ." Ruby said slowly.

"Well, Doug came up to visit me. He had a hotel room for the weekend. We walked up and down the waterfront and had a wonderful time. We went out to dinner,

and it was not charity. It was romantic.
We returned to the hotel, and even though
people watched us as we made our way
to his room, I did not care. Doug came all
this way to see me, and we were going to
continue catching up." Liz paused.

"Go on," Ruby urged.

"I did not realize how much fun Doug
is . . . and guess what? Never mind, I will
tell you." Liz sucked in a deep breath and
continued. "He moved back to Wisconsin
and is running his granddad's dairy farm. He
said he just loves working in the fresh air
and taking care of the farm. He told me the
dairy farm is very successful. From what
he said, I think he is quite the businessman
when it comes to selling his milk in town and
surrounding areas."

Ruby held her breath and waited for Liz
to continue.

"Ruby, Doug told me that he could not
get me out of his head, even after all this
time." Liz sighed. "Well, one thing led to
another, and the next thing I knew"—Liz
lowered her voice—"we slept together."

Ruby gasped.

A spark lit up Liz's eyes, and her voice
was pure happiness. "Oh, Ruby, it was magic.
I knew when I started kissing him that it

was true love. My body was on fire, and I could not get enough of him. When it was all over, well, I had never felt so alive. Ruby, it was my first time, I swear! He is truly the bee's knees!"

"OK. Then what happened?"

"We agreed to keep seeing each other. We have been exchanging letters. He writes the most romantic letters."

"OK . . . and?"

"Well, I missed my period. I think I am PG," whispered Liz. "I wrote and told Doug. He wants to get married right away." Liz's voice rose in excitement.

"Oh, my!" Ruby said. "What about your job?"

"I've thought about that," said Liz. "I will get another one when I move back home. Doug is fine with me working, and he said he would pay for a cleaning lady once a week— that is how much money he is making!"

"And what about the baby? If you work, who will care for the baby?"

"I have not worked that out yet." Liz scowled. "I need you to be happy for me."

"Are you happy?"

"I am thrilled."

"Then, I am happy for you too." Ruby hugged her friend. "So now what?"

"Well, I was going to tell Mr. Wiess today, but when he shared the office news, I thought I should wait another day."

"Well, I think you should tell him as soon as possible."

"I know," Liz agreed.

"When do you want to move?" Ruby asked.

"Well, we thought we would go to the justice of the peace this coming weekend, so no one needs to know that we had to get married but you. It isn't like my parents are forcing him to. Doug asked me," Liz added.

Ruby shook her head. "Of course," she said. "I totally understand." She placed her hand on Liz's to reassure her.

"Ruby, will you come and be our witness?"

"Absolutely!"

"Thank you! You just wait till you meet 'the one.' You'll understand why I just couldn't help myself. I had to give in to my passion!"

Ruby smiled. "I hope there is a Mr. Special for me out there."

"Sure, there is," Liz said. "It happens when you least expect it. You wait and see!"

Ruby smiled and waved to Jo that they were ready for the check. The girls paid their bill, left Jo a tip, and made their way to the streetcars to head home. Ruby watched the traffic and the hustle and bustle of people and other streetcars passing each other. It was a constant stream, there were so many. Chicago was known for having the largest streetcar system in the nation.

As Ruby rode the streetcar home, she let her mind wander in the Ruby fashion. *Oh, my. Secrets were definitely revealed*, she thought to herself as she shook her head and grinned. *But Liz's secret was the most important news of all! At least when I get home, I can just relax and be glad I am not pregnant. But, Liz is happy and that's what's important.*

Mrs. Clark greeted Ruby when she came in the door. Ruby was often not home for supper, but Mrs. Clark always had a warm plate. She treated Ruby as if she were her daughter.

This evening was a little different. Ruby could tell Mrs. Clark was excited about the mail as she handed it over. Ruby saw who it was from and immediately understood why Mrs. Clark seemed so curious. Ruby assured her that Arthur was not a boyfriend, or as

Mrs. Clark's generation referred to a man of interest, a "beau."

Ruby knew there were times when Mrs. Clark worried about Ruby and other girls of her generation becoming spinsters. On many occasions, Ruby had to assure her that things were changing, and men and women liked knowing a girl or guy before they walked down an aisle and said "I do." On one occasion, Mrs. Clark shared how her parents introduced her to Tom, who wound up being the perfect match. They learned about each other, and their friendship grew into love. Ruby shared with Mrs. Clark how not everyone is that lucky. Mrs. Clark just patted Ruby on the knee and said, "Yes, dear, you are right," and the conversation ended.

After supper, Ruby helped Mrs. Clark with the dishes as usual but could not wait to get upstairs and read what Arthur had to say. She could not imagine why he had written, as Arthur had barely spoken to her when she moved back home after college.

Finally, Ruby hung up her apron, gave Mrs. Clark a kiss good night, and ran upstairs to her room.

Dear Ruby,

I heard you finally made it to Chicago, and you are doing very well for yourself. I am sorry we did not see each other when you were in town—I was not ready to see you. It would have brought back many memories, and I would have found myself thinking about what might have been. So, without dredging up old history, I have some news that I hope you will find to be good news. I finally realized you were right, and I started seeing a new girl in town. Maggie Garrett. She is lovely, and we will be married in a few weeks. We thought right before Christmas would be a perfect time so that we can start the New Year as man and wife. December 15 is the wedding date, and I wanted you to know before someone in your family told you. I am not sure if it even matters to you, but I felt I should be the one to tell you.

So, that is my news. I can officially close our chapter and thank you for the memories. I hope you will stop in the hardware store and meet Maggie when you are in town. She runs the cash register. We make a great team *at the store, and I am sure we will be happy as man and wife. I hope you find what you are looking for in the big world out there.*

Warm regards,
Arthur

Ruby placed the letter in her journal and quietly prepared for bed.

The next morning over breakfast, Ruby updated Mrs. Clark. Ruby knew she would be curious and thought she would save Mrs. Clark the trouble of wondering what the letter might contain.

Mrs. Clark nodded as Ruby shared what was in the letter. When Ruby finished, she folded her hands in her lap.

"Do you have any regrets, my dear?" Mrs. Clark asked.

"Well, one can always wonder, can't one?" she replied. "But I know I'm on the right path for me." She smiled. "I do hope to marry one day, but I want to engage in the business world and see where it takes me first."

Mrs. Clark hugged Ruby and said, "You young girls, you are so strong! I am proud of you, Ruby. Just remember one thing—go after your dreams, but keep in mind, there is a lid for every pot out there, and your lid will show up one day."

Ruby looked puzzled for a moment and then finally realized what the pot and lid were, chuckled, hugged Mrs. Clark, and left for work.

Ruby had told the Clarks that she was going to be a witness for Liz's big day, and Mr. Clark agreed to drive Ruby to the justice of the peace. He knew she was going to a late lunch with the bride and groom and two other witnesses who would see Ruby home. Ruby was appreciative of the ride because it was bitterly cold. Mr. Clark commented that for December, it was an unseasonably warm day and should bring good luck to the couple. Ruby had noticed the temperature gauge on the wall while putting on her coat and thought, *Twenty-nine degrees, not warm.*

"Well, there you are, Ruby." Mr. Clark turned to her as he pulled up. "You best get inside before it gets any colder."

Ruby thanked him and made her way into
the building.

It was a small white structure that
looked like a mini church. Ruby entered the
wet room and a chime went off to let the
office staff know someone had arrived. A
lady greeted her and showed Ruby where to
hang her things and put her wet boots, then
walked her into the next room, where Liz was
waiting for her.

"Oh, Ruby, you are here!" Liz exclaimed
as she hugged her.

"Of course, dear, why wouldn't I be?"
Ruby let out a giggle.

"Oh, I don't know why I said that," Liz
said. "I guess I'm just a bit nervous."

"You are not having second thoughts, are
you?" asked Ruby.

"No, I just . . . well . . ." She paused.
"Ruby, no one knows our secret, right?"

"Of course not. Now stop worrying," Ruby
said and patted Liz's arm. "You are about to
get married and start a new chapter in your
life." She took her hand. "Now let's get
you hitched!"

"Right!" Liz smiled at Ruby.

Just then, there was a knock on the
door, and the greeter said it was Liz's turn.
Ruby had never been in a chapel before

and realized from the woman's comment
that several weddings took place there in
a day, unlike church weddings where the
most might be two—one in the morning and
maybe one in the evening. In Oilton, a church
would dedicate the entire weekend to the
wedding party.

The two girls looked at each other, and
Ruby straightened the white netting on
Liz's hat.

"Oh, I almost forgot." Ruby opened a
small plastic case and pulled out a corsage
made of tiny pink roses with baby's breath
around them. She pinned it on Liz's white,
tailored suit. "There, you look perfect."

Liz glanced in the mirror one more time,
smoothing down her top and making sure her
wrist-length white gloves with the white
pearl-shaped buttons were on snug. She
checked her stockings for runs and made sure
the lines going up the back of her legs were
straight. The white pumps on her petite feet
completed her outfit.

The greeter was beginning to get impatient
and reminded them that the minister had
more weddings to do that day. The girls
giggled and followed her. They stopped in
front of the red arched double doors.

"Where are the men?" Liz's eyes darted around the foyer.

"They're waiting inside for you," the greeter assured her. "My husband and I try and make it as much like a church wedding as possible," she continued. "Now stand up straight. Ruby, you will walk up first, then the bride will follow. Ruby, you turn off to the left." She waved her hand to one side. "And Liz, you stand in the center up front, and the groom will join you. Got it?" She helped straighten Liz's corsage. "Now, remember I will be taking pictures; you will have your moment preserved. So, before you walk down the aisle, you wait, and I will take your photo, and then you can leave the chapel. The groom knows this too. Got it?"

The girls nodded their heads, and the woman opened the door and went in and closed the door behind her. She then opened it just enough to give a thumbs-up and left it open for them to follow.

The wedding march began, and Ruby found herself walking up a small aisle to the altar. She felt very awkward, especially when she saw Mr. Wiess and Doug smiling. She knew it was not because of her, but the feeling was so strange that she blushed. Ruby did not realize that Liz was not walking right behind her. Ruby saw the parents of the bride and groom in the pews, and they were smiling too. When Ruby took her place, Liz was given the cue to begin walking up the aisle. Ruby smiled with happiness as she watched Liz having her moment as a bride and Doug beaming as the wedding march played on.

Liz joined Doug, and the justice of the peace began the ceremony. Ruby half listened as she wondered what she would do without her friend, who always had her back. Now Liz was leaving for a new life and was over the moon about it. As Ruby watched them exchange rings, she wondered what life would be like for Liz and prayed it was everything she hoped it would be. The ceremony seemed to go very fast, and before she knew it, Ruby heard the words "I now pronounce you man and wife." And just like that, Liz and Doug were married.

The couple kissed, turned around for their picture, and walked down the aisle. Ruby, Mr. Wiess, the justice of the peace, and both sets of parents followed. Once out of the chapel, there were many handshakes and congratulations. Everyone hugged each other, and Mr. Wiess handed the justice of the

peace an envelope with what Ruby assumed
was a tip inside.

Mr. Wiess had three cars waiting for
the wedding party: one for the bride and
groom, one for Ruby, Mr. Wiess, and Roger
Williams, the groom's best friend, and one
for the couple's parents. The wedding party
went to the new Shoreland Hotel in the
upscale Hyde Park neighborhood; it had
just opened in May. Mr. Wiess said that
Liz was such a dedicated employee and he
hated to see her go. He decided to show
his appreciation for her work. He wanted to
send her and her new husband off in style,
and what better place than the upscale
hotel? Mr. Wiess surprised the couple with
a wedding gift and a honeymoon night at the
hotel before they made their way to dairy
farm country in Wisconsin.

The Shoreland was the talk of the town with
its thirteen floors and one thousand guest
rooms. Many elite families held weddings
and receptions in the large banquet hall and
crystal ballroom.

Mr. Wiess had reserved a table for the
wedding party. A long table in the Shoreland

Restaurant was decorated for the bride and groom. Liz could not have been happier, and the wedding party had a grand time. Mr. Wiess even ordered champagne and toasted the happy couple.

Ruby took it all in and thought again, *Too bad he is my boss. He is everything a girl would want—progressive in his thoughts toward women working, attends church on Sunday, thoughtful, and a successful businessman.* For the first time, Ruby wondered if Mr. Wiess had a special girl in his life. She could not help but wonder as she sat directly across from him. There were times she felt him looking at her and found herself looking back. She knew he had noticed she had been staring at him, and she could feel a flush building on her cheeks.

"Are you having a good time?" Mr. Wiess began, making polite conversation.

"Oh, yes, thank you," Ruby replied and turned to hear what others were saying.

"Are you enjoying your steak?" he asked.

Ruby pretended not to hear the question. "I'm sorry, I didn't hear you. Can you repeat the question?" Ruby was trying to be coy, not wanting him to know she was praying he would strike up a conversation.

He repeated the question with a smirk.

Ruby stuttered and said how much she enjoyed steak and then found herself talking about her mother's cooking and how her mom would soak the steak in milk for a few hours for tenderness and then season it before she would cook it over a wood fire.

She realized he was enjoying her stories, so she relaxed a bit. From then on, the two continued to enjoy their meal, deep in conversation as if no one else were around them.

The meal was followed by toasts to the lovely couple and then one more surprise from Mr. Wiess—a stunning two-layer wedding cake! The couple thanked him, Doug shook Mr. Wiess's hand, and Liz hugged him. The happy couple laughed while cutting the unexpected but very appreciated cake and fed each other the first bite.

Eventually, the party wound up, and Ruby found herself hugging her best friend goodbye. Before she knew it, she was accepting a ride home with Mr. Wiess.

As she got in his car, Ruby was uncomfortable and started talking about the weather. Mr. Wiess smiled and asked her about her family, which immediately put her at ease. The tense atmosphere disappeared once Ruby started talking about her momma and dad and the big plans the men of Oilton had for their town.

When they arrived at the Clarks', Ruby started to open the door, but Mr. Wiess insisted he open it for her. She appreciated it very much, and as he straightened her coat around her neck, he told her he would walk her to the door. Ruby looked at him and wanted to melt as the butterflies in her stomach—which she had not felt since she was a young girl kissing under the bleachers after a high school football game—returned.

Ruby knew she needed to get inside quickly before her face gave her away. There was this moment, and she knew they both felt it as Mr. Wiess looked into Ruby's eyes. Then he seemed to shake it off and walked her to the door like a gentleman. Ruby noticed Mrs. Clark peering through the lace curtains and then quickly stepping away when she saw them getting closer. Once at the door, Ruby promptly reached out to shake hands with her boss so as not to give him the impression there would be another moment.

"Thank you so much for a lovely evening and for the ride home, Mr. Wiess."

He looked at her, smiled, and shook his head.

"Ruby, we are not at work, so you may call me John."

"Oh, I don't know." Ruby shuffled her feet and dug in her purse for her key.

"Please, I insist."

"Right, OK, John. Thank you and good night." She forced a smile.

"Great. Good night, Ruby." He turned and walked to his car.

Ruby stood there for a moment, then unlocked the door and quickly went inside.

Ruby plugged in the kettle and poured tea for herself and Mrs. Clark, who she knew would be waiting for details. They sat in the kitchen, teacups in hand, and Ruby shared details on the entire wedding from start to finish. Mrs. Clark kept nodding in encouragement for Ruby to continue.

Finally, Ruby made her way to her room. As she lay in bed, she thought about the details she had not shared with Mrs. Clark—her dinner exchange with her boss.

Ruby thought of his eyes and how she noticed a gentleness in them. She sighed as she thought of his kindness and generosity toward her. But she shook herself out of her daze when she started to wonder if he had a chest covered with a thick layer of chestnut-brown hair, like he had on his head. She and her friends always thought men with lots of chest hair were very sexy. Once her mind went there, her body began to tingle all over, and Ruby became flushed and needed to make those thoughts disappear. She could not go down that rabbit hole with her imagination and knew most certainly she would not want to date her boss. With that last thought, Ruby fell asleep.

Chapter 7

NOTHING STAYS THE SAME

DECEMBER 1926 (PART 2)

"What do you mean you are leaving?" Ruby asked Helen as they were getting their coats in the locker room, preparing to go home for the day.

"Well, I've been thinking about it ever since you received your promotion."

Helen explained how she wanted to be more than a secretary. She wanted to learn more, so she had begun watching for job opportunities. She told Ruby that Max Mason, the new president at the University of Chicago, was looking for an executive assistant.

"And I landed the job," she said. "I know I am going to be learning so much."

Helen continued to talk about the responsibility a university president had. Ruby had never seen Helen this excited before. She went on to talk about how she would know things going on in different departments, especially in medicine. Ruby let Helen chatter on about how the new president had big dreams for the university. Helen became background noise as Ruby looked for something in her purse.

Suddenly, Helen stopped talking. Ruby looked up and gave her a puzzled look.

Helen continued, "Ruby, I have you to thank for this move."

"Me? How on earth?" Ruby was very surprised to hear those words.

"Well, because of your story," Helen replied. "You took a job, had a plan, and never gave up until you were working in the field you wanted. You gave me the courage to see what else I could do, and I will never forget you." She finished buttoning her coat. "Let's try and stay in touch, shall we?"

Helen gave Ruby a wave and, with that, was out the door.

Ruby put on her coat, hat, and gloves and left the building, bracing for the bitter December wind. Heading home on the streetcar, she thought about Helen and

the fun times with the other girls. She had
not seen the girls in weeks, as she was
committed to her new position and never
really had time to make it up to her old
floor. Even when she went to the ladies'
room, it was a different set of women, and
Ruby did not see a need to socialize with
them. Instead, she focused on making sure
the men knew that when she left her desk
for the powder room, she would not be
wasting time with idle chatter. Ruby loved
her new job and never thought about missing
out on what was going on in her friends'
lives. Once home, she had a chance to share
with Mrs. Clark the events of the day.

Ruby now felt part of the Clark family.
She was grateful to them for taking her
in. Ruby wanted to be part of the business
world, but she still wanted a family. She
knew that every town had its rough side—the
oil riggers and the bandits in Oilton, and
the mobs in Chicago—and because of this,
she welcomed Mr. Clark's connection to the
town as a Freemason. It also made her feel
that her dad was somehow watching over her.

Ruby did not like seeing the dark side
of people. She once told Mrs. Clark that
she could not understand gangs; they just
needed to be taught proper behavior by their

parents. Mrs. Clark tried to explain, but Ruby's rose-colored glasses stayed firmly in place, and she was not ready to give them up.

The Clarks were pleased with Ruby's company. Even though Mr. Clark worked, he was not around younger employees, and Ruby helped the Clarks stay connected with the ideas of the younger generation. At suppertime, Ruby shared Helen's news and how excited she was for her. Mr. Clark was impressed with Helen's new job as Ruby shared the details with him.

When Mrs. Clark and Ruby were cleaning up, Ruby shared how much things were changing already. Liz was married, Helen was changing jobs, friends from college were all married now, and Ruby did not have time to visit the other secretaries on her former floor. Mrs. Clark was a good listener and kept quiet until Ruby finished her monologue.

With the last plate put away for the night, Mrs. Clark turned to her. "Ruby, I have an idea, but only if you are in the mood to hear it." She paused and folded her dish towel. "I learned from my daughter a long time ago that sometimes people want you to just listen, not tell them how to fix things."

Ruby nodded. She was open to hearing her thoughts.

Mrs. Clark smiled. "OK then, here goes. I don't think you should worry. Things have a way of working themselves out. People you meet move on just like you moved on from your town, then from college. It is part of life. Now you must think about where you want life to take you. Think of ways to branch out from work and meet other people, like perhaps the women's group at church." She paused and let her words sink in. "I hope that is helpful advice, Now, you go on; I will finish down here."

Ruby gave her a hug good night and said she would sleep on it.

The winter wind was howling as Ruby put on her thick, warm flannel nightgown and crawled into bed. She thought about how lucky she was to be independent yet safe in a family home. Ruby smiled as she thought about Mrs. Clark's ideas.

That Sunday at Grace United Methodist Church in Logan Square, Ruby joined the women's group where she met women of various ages, including a girl named Zoe.

The church group supported people who needed help with clothing and food. At the moment, the greatest need was for blankets. Ruby found helping others was second nature, as she used to do similar charity work with her momma.

Back at work, things were going great guns. Ruby was surprised at how well the men at work treated her and how much they respected her. One day, Mr. Wiess called Ruby into his office at the end of the day. He reported that she was doing a fine job in the accounting department. Of course, Ruby was pleased, and before Mr. Wiess could offer her a ride home, she thanked him, excused herself, and quickly made her way to the streetcar.

Ruby had had those butterflies once more and knew she had needed to get out of his office before she blushed. As she made her way home, Ruby reflected on the glowing report Mr. White had given about her to Mr. Wiess. Ruby had read articles about how many men did not value their female coworkers, no matter how good of a job they did. Her new friend, Zoe, had shared

how men at her own office tried to make
advances toward some of the women who
worked there, even if they were married.
Ruby was so involved in her thoughts she
almost missed her stop, and she quickly made
her way off the streetcar just in time before
it took off again.

The workweek passed quickly, with Ruby
punching in numbers and double-checking the
various customer accounts. She was learning
a lot about business and her core work. Mr.
White was pleased to give her insight into
different companies. He appreciated Ruby
and saw her as an asset, relieving him of
some of the workload so he could leave work
at a reasonable hour and enjoy time with his
family in the evenings.

Saturday was freezing, and Ruby saw no
reason to be outside; she knew she would
have to go out on Sunday. So, she stayed
inside, helped around the house, and enjoyed
reading and writing letters home. The Clarks
were used to the weather, and they didn't
mind going out, allowing Ruby to putter
around the house in peace. Ruby decided
to surprise them when they came home and

made her momma's chocolate brownies. The
Clarks both had a sweet tooth, so they
were happy to have this treat there when
they returned.

Later in the afternoon, Ruby decided
to bundle up and go out to dinner with
Zoe. The conversation flowed from topic
to topic, from various work situations, to
politics, and most notably, men. The two
girls saw eye to eye on every issue, and the
friendship blossomed.

Zoe had moved to Chicago from Nebraska.
She had this urge to see the big city but
did not want to be clear across the country
in New York if she needed to get home to
her parents. The train ride from Chicago to
Nebraska was an easy trip, and she shared
with Ruby how she liked the idea that home
was only a train ride away.

They talked about how amazed they were
to see the Wrigley Building and the Tribune
Tower for the first time. The girls enjoyed
discussing the architecture in Chicago, and
they both appreciated the Chicago Board
of Trade Building. They were amazed that
as early as 1885, people were able to build
a tower that was 320 feet tall with a large
clock, a 4,500-pound bell, and a nine-foot
copper weather vane in the shape of a ship.

Ruby told Zoe that she had read that when they turned on the light in the tower for the first time, people could see the light over sixty miles away. The girls agreed—how could you not love to work in a city like Chicago! They decided that Ruby's first Christmas in Chicago had to be magical, as Zoe shared how it always was for her.

In the days leading up to Christmas, Ruby buried herself in work and wanted to have all the accounting done for year-end, but more importantly, to enjoy the holidays.

It was the season of goodwill, and Ruby and Zoe got into the spirit by helping Mrs. Clark make Christmas cards for her close friends. The girls made a few for themselves to hand out as well. Ruby even made one for her parents; she knew her momma would enjoy the fact that she had made the card. Zoe then went home to be with her family.

On Christmas Day, Ruby called home, and the family was having fun, especially with all the grandkids. Ruby knew her parents'

lives were busy with day-to-day family and business activities. During the conversation, she made the mistake of telling her sister she missed everyone. Well, that gave Rilla an invitation to tell Ruby it was her fault. Rilla then told Ruby the family was busy and she need not take up any more of their momma's time and hung up. Ruby just looked at the phone in shock and hurt. She did not even get to ask her momma how she liked her Christmas card. Ruby regained her composure before rejoining everyone in the Clarks' family room. After Ruby spoke with her family, the Clarks' children had called and were grateful to Ruby for being with their parents.

Ruby enjoyed the few days off during the holidays, and Mrs. Clark enjoyed teaching her how to make bread and a light crust for pies. Ruby had become more receptive to learning how to cook than when she was a young girl. She now saw the need to cook for friends and herself. Ruby knew her momma would be proud that she finally knew how to use an oven.

After the baking lesson, Ruby adjourned

to her room, where she wrote in her journal. She thought about Helen and the other girls she had met. Liz was busy with her new life, and Helen had a new job and a man in her life. Mabel and Margaret had both moved on to new jobs and had not stayed in touch with anyone. Louise was the only one still content working for the insurance company. For the first time, Ruby said out loud, "I'm ready to share my life." Before Zoe had left for Nebraska, the two girls had made plans to have a bit of fun and get all the girls together when she returned in the New Year. Ruby closed her journal and bid it good night.

Chapter 8

THINGS ARE NOT LOOKING UP

MARCH—DECEMBER 1927

As Ruby packed to move, she recalled how her momma always said, "Life happens in the blink of an eye." She had never realized the power of the phrase until that moment. It was time for her to move out of the Clarks', and it was a sad time for everyone. Mr. Clark had been in a car accident and had not survived. Mrs. Clark had sold the house, and the next day was moving day for her too. Mrs. Clark would be moving in with her daughter, Sarah, and her grandkids. Ruby realized that life sure could change at

a moment's notice. Her heart ached for the
Clark family.

Mrs. Clark had sold almost everything in
her home and was only having a few things
moved to her daughter's home. It did not
take long for the moving company to load
the truck, as it was basically only what Mrs.
Clark would have in her new room.

They watched the moving truck head off,
and Ruby looked over at Mrs. Clark and saw
the pain on her face. They walked slowly
back inside one last time. A few smaller
bags were in the living room. Mrs. Clark's
things would go in Sarah's car, and Ruby's
things went into the car that belonged to
the neighbors, Mr. and Mrs. Romano. They
had volunteered to take Ruby to the rooming
house where she would be living. Ruby
hugged Mrs. Clark and told her she would
write. And with that, Ruby and the Romanos
drove away.

Ruby knew the Romanos from church,
and they had helped her find a place in a
rooming house.

They wished they had room for her, but

they didn't, and on short notice Ruby was lucky to get this room.

When they arrived, they were greeted by Mrs. Oakes, the house mother. None of them had ever been inside a rooming house before, and they all took in their surroundings. Ruby was shown to her room on the second floor. It took two trips to get all of Ruby's things in the room even though she really did not have that much. The Romanos hugged Ruby.

"We will see you at church." Mrs. Romano gave Ruby's arm a squeeze. "Let us know if you need anything at all, my dear."

"Thank you both for all your help. I'll be just fine," Ruby said with a bravado she didn't quite feel.

Ruby closed the door behind them and turned to look around. For the first time, she realized how hard most single working women had it; she realized to a greater degree just how much she had been spoiled by living with the Clarks, especially rent free. She took in the contents of her new accommodations, which had just the bare necessities—not even a wardrobe, only a wire string across the wall to hang her clothes on. There was no window to let in any fresh air, but she saw she had a tiny desk, a chair, and a single bed. Lucky for Ruby, Mrs. Clark had given

her some linen for her new place. She didn't
have a kitchen so to speak, but she did have
a counter in the corner with a single burner
to heat up food.

After Ruby had unpacked, Mrs. Oakes
showed her where the bathrooms were
located. Mrs. Oakes explained how the
showers worked and told Ruby her shower
time for Monday was at five in the morning,
and each shower should only be five minutes.
Timings were on a rotational basis to be fair
for everyone. There were two bathrooms and
ten rooms on each floor.

Ruby was then shown to the dining hall in
the basement. It was pretty bleak, with only
tables and chairs; however, they did provide
basic food. Mrs. Oakes was proud to say
they either had coffee or water for breakfast
along with a piece of toast. There was no
lunch, but for dinner, they had hot stew or a
soup of some sort.

Ruby returned to her room and sat on
the end of her bed, wishing there could have
been a room available in a nicer place, like
where her friends lived. Ruby stood up and
plugged in the phonograph Mrs. Clark had

given her as a going-away present. Not too long after the music began playing, there was a knock on her door. Ruby opened it to a frowning house mother.

"I know you're new here," began Mrs. Oakes, "but we reserve the use of our electricity for more important things, certainly not a personal phonograph." She sniffed and nodded in the direction of the offending noisemaker. "If you are smart, you will hide it. No one is used to a person who can afford such things living in a rooming house." With another huff, she walked away.

Ruby turned off her music and once more sat on the bed and looked at her surroundings. She shook her head and looked at her phonograph sitting on the floor of her sparsely appointed room. Where would she even hide it? Ruby mumbled to herself, "How did the world go so topsy-turvy? What was I thinking when my parents offered to help me find a place to live, and I turned them down? Why on earth did I say, 'Thank you, but it is time I learn to stand on my own'?" She sighed, realizing that had been before she knew what a rooming house really was. She bet her parents knew and did not say a word. She felt slightly better that at least she had put her name on a waiting list for the

Eleanor Club, where her friend Zoe lived. For now, she would make do. At least she had a roof over her head.

Monday morning came, and there was no Mrs. Clark with breakfast ready or a snack to take to work. She took a cold shower and got dressed. Ruby had farther to travel to work now on her new streetcar route, so she left early in case she messed up.

Several weeks passed, and by the time spring approached, Ruby had gotten the hang of her new route. One thing she had not adjusted to was the shower schedule. It was such a pain. It was always changing, and some girls forgot their time, which caused problems. If anyone complained, they risked getting into a physical fight. One morning Ruby saw one going on as she was walking down the hall toward the showers and quickly turned around and headed back to her room. There was no shower that day.

One evening after work, Ruby went to the diner across from her office, where all

her good fortune first took place. She had
not been there for some time, and she just
wanted to put off going back to the dreary
rooming house and her lonely room. Jo was
still waitressing there and recognized Ruby.
They caught up in between Jo taking orders
and working the tables.

Ruby told her the year had started out
great celebrating the New Year quietly
at Zoe's place with a few friends, as it
would not have been wise to be on the
streets on New Year's Eve. However, they
had then gone out the following weekend,
and the world had turned upside down.
Ruby told Jo how she moved and why. Jo
was a good listener and loved to hear her
customers' stories.

In the midst of Ruby's storytelling, Jo
sighed. "Wait a minute, dear, I will be right
back." She waited on her next customer and
then returned with Ruby's dinner. "There you
go, my dear, and I have some thoughts for
you." She told Ruby how life has its ups and
downs. "You have had some good luck," she
said. "So now you've had a bit of bad luck,
you just must keep your chin up till things go
your way again. That is how I look at life."
She gave Ruby's shoulder a squeeze.

Ruby smiled and agreed, though she had

never had it this rough before. Ruby finished her meal, left a tip, and thanked Jo for the advice. It was just what she needed.

For the next while, Ruby buried herself in work and in writing letters back in her room but slacked off on writing in her journal. It was depressing to report what she was up to, which was nothing. Nothing cheered Ruby up—not even watching more skyscrapers being built.

Ruby was watching every penny, as this was the first time she had ever paid rent or even paid for her meals. On occasion, she had tried give money to the Clarks for food, but they would not take it. They told her they never wanted her to feel like a boarder, and they were right; they had made her feel like family.

One evening Ruby finally picked up her journal and wrote:

> *If it was not for my letters to and from Mrs. Clark as well as Momma, I might go MAD. I am always counting my pennies, and I find I am not even going to church to help out with the*

Ruby closed her journal and lay down in her bed, wishing for life to get better, and finally fell asleep with tears running down her face.

Several more weeks went by, and Ruby had not heard from any of her friends. Work was not as enjoyable anymore. One of the accountants had been let go, and the workload increased for everyone. Ruby thought for sure when the evaluations came around, she would be up for a raise, so that was something to look forward to. She was super excited for her meeting scheduled with

Mr. Wiess. She had not seen him for some
time and made sure she wore her Sunday
best for the meeting that could change
her life.

Mr. Wiess was more businesslike than
ever before when he asked Ruby to come in
his office, close the door, and take a seat.
There was not even a hint of a smile, and
Ruby felt a cold chill in the air.

"It is good to see you," he began, "and I
hear you are doing a fine job in accounting.
I know you have taken on a larger workload,
and I wish I could offer you a large increase
in pay, but unfortunately, I can't." He
paused. "But Mr. White and I agree that you
should be recognized and rewarded for your
extra work. We discussed giving you a title
of assistant head accountant, along with a
five-cent-a-day pay increase. I know this is
not much of a bump, but the title will look
good for you in the future."

Ruby was silent, so Mr. Wiess continued.

"I'm sure you will hear some of the
men received a bigger raise, but they have
families, and that means more mouths to
feed." He shuffled some papers from one
side of his desk to the other. "I hope you
understand our decision. We believe your new
title is reasonable compensation. Well, that

will be all, and thank you for your dedication
to the job."

Ruby looked at him and knew if she said
what was on her mind, she could be out
the door. So, she thanked him and returned
to work.

When she entered the accounting office,
her colleagues started clapping, and Mr.
White presented her with a nameplate
for her desk that said "Assistant Head
Accountant." Everyone congratulated her
and then Mr. White asked everyone to get
back to work.

As Ruby made her way home, she was
down in the dumps. She had a new title,
which was good, but she still did not have
equal pay, which made her mad even though
she knew no woman ever got paid as much as
a man. Regardless, the extra money would
come in handy when a room became available
at the Eleanor Club. Ruby returned to her
room and before falling asleep decided she
would make use of her new title to start
looking for another job.

Over the ensuing weeks, Ruby's parents
offered to help her out again, and she

refused on principle. One evening, Ruby
received a call from the Eleanor Club that
a room had opened up if she wanted it,
beginning in the New Year. There was no
question that Ruby wanted it, and she said
so and hung up the phone. She did a little
dance, went downstairs to give her notice,
hugged a stunned Mrs. Oakes, and hummed
all the way back to her room.

The following months did not seem so
depressing, as Ruby had something to look
forward to. On New Year's Eve, Ruby wrote
in her journal while sitting on her bed at the
rooming house one last time.

Dear Journal,

*Finally, I think my luck is about to
change! I am moving to the Eleanor
Club tomorrow, January 1, 1928. This
has been the hardest year of my life,
yet now that I look back on it, I
realize it has been a year of growth.
I had no idea I had the strength to
make it through, but I did. One nice
thing about not going out is you do
a lot of reading, and I have learned
about some wonderful people making
a difference in the world who I want*

to be sure I remember. Like Elizabeth Lindsay Davis, a Black woman who founded the Phyllis Wheatley Women's Club. An inspiring leader of not only the women's movement, but also in empowering other young African American women. It's what I enjoy most about Chicago. People are always fighting for their rights, learning, inventing, and moving the country forward.

Even though it was a tough year, it was one of firsts. Charles Lindbergh successfully flew from New York to Paris; Babe Ruth hit his 60th home run; weather maps are being broadcast on television; and the first transatlantic telephone call was made. It gives me hope for the future!

On a personal note, I have not been back to see Momma and Dad in two years, and no one has been up here either. Traveling to other states takes a long time, it is costly, and my married siblings have their responsibilities at home. What I miss most in the winter are Momma's warm biscuits and gravy; and when she adds sausage, well, it such comfort food.

I know I'm rambling, but on another topic, President Calvin Coolidge continues to be popular, especially with his tax cuts. I am reading a lot about that in the newspaper. I read a lot! My two favorite books are *Tomorrow Morning* and *Lost Ecstasy*.

I heard about the movie *The Jazz Singer*. The film is part silent and part sound. It is incredible how far technology has come. Think about it, in my lifetime I have seen us go from horses to automobiles, photography has improved, more people have indoor plumbing, now silent picture movies are becoming talkies, and we can make phone calls across the Atlantic and fly a plane across it too—and that is to only name a few things. No telling what inventors will think of next.

Well, that about wraps up 1927. The most important thing is my family back home are all well, and my friends here are all healthy. But finally, I don't think I will ever get used to this cold weather. Sometimes, I think my toes and hands will never warm up, they stay purple and blue for so long. I have to keep rubbing them to

get the blood flowing, and then all is
well! Good night for now, and goodbye
to 1927.

Chapter 9

COMING INTO HER OWN

JANUARY 1928

A new day, a new year, and moving day had arrived! Ruby was overjoyed as Zoe helped her with the move and getting settled in. Ruby was thrilled to be closer to her friend, that she did not have to get up so early to get to work, and most of all, she had a window and a closet for her things.

Ruby started her search for a new job, which took several weeks, but finally she heard about an opening at one of her favorite shopping spots: The Fair. She applied for it, and she landed it. Mr. Wiess had been right; the new title of assistant head accountant paid off. She was offered a higher salary than her counterparts at the insurance company. Ruby handed in her notice, and before January was even over, she had started her new job. Ruby felt her life was right side up again.

Even though Zoe and Ruby lived in the same building, they were both so busy with their work, and with Ruby starting a new job, it was harder to find time to catch up. One day, Ruby saw Zoe long enough to tell her the good news. Zoe was overjoyed for her, and they agreed that it was a cause for celebration. Zoe knew Ruby had not been out in a good while, so she said the Green Mill was the place to go, and Ruby agreed. They planned to meet there, as Ruby had some things she needed to do before heading out.

Zoe had not even seen Ruby's new do! She had given into the bob look with waves added to her auburn hair. Ruby felt more grown-up than ever before, a confident businesswoman who enjoyed jazz music with her friends. The girls still had to be careful not to be seen going to a speakeasy, as Prohibition was still running strong.

When Ruby arrived at the back door, she

waved at Zoe, who almost did not recognize her. Once inside, Zoe made a fuss over her new look, which made Ruby feel more carefree than ever before.

"What made you chop off your beautiful long hair?" Zoe fluffed the back of Ruby's hair.

"Oh, it was time I came into my own," Ruby said. "I have not been to the beauty parlor in a year, and I wanted to treat myself." Ruby laughed. "The hairdresser made a comment about how much easier my hair would be to take care of if I had it in a bob, and I thought, 'Oh why not?'"

"Well, it suits you," Zoe said.

"I sure hope so," Ruby replied. "It cost a whopping five dollars, but I needed a pick-me-up after the year from you-know-where."

The girls laughed.

"Let's drink to that," said Zoe, and she called the waiter over to order drinks.

The band came out, and the girls realized The MacDougall Band was back. It was the same band that Ruby had seen the last time she was there. The music began, and people started dancing while Zoe and Ruby listened and enjoyed their drinks.

After a while, the girls were asked to dance. Ruby was afraid of losing their table,

but the men convinced her not to worry, and
they all hit the dance floor.

After a few songs, Zoe left the dance
floor, so Ruby followed, and they returned
to their table. The two men they had been
dancing with joined the girls at their table
and seemed to be having a good time till
they realized their advances were not taking
them where they wanted, and they shoved
off. Ruby was happy to see them leave, as
she was dying to speak to Zoe in private.
Once the men left, she scooted her chair
closer to Zoe so she could hear her over
the band.

"Zoe, did you notice the clarinet player?"
Zoe started to answer, but Ruby continued.
"Well, every time I did a turn on the dance
floor, it seemed he was looking right at me.
But, of course, I must be imagining things.
I never met him, and I danced with Harold
all night."

Zoe craned her neck to see. "Oh yes, he's
a looker for sure." She winked at Ruby.

The girls finished their drinks and
decided it was time to head home to the
Eleanor Club.

Ruby chatted the whole way home about the clarinet player, her move into the new place, and her new job.

Zoe finally got a word in edgewise. "I'm still shocked that you can dance so well."

They went inside, and Zoe followed Ruby into her room and insisted that Ruby explain herself. Ruby felt it was too late to go into it all, but Zoe was persistent.

Ruby gave in and made a cup of tea to help them stay awake. She brought it to Zoe and sat next to her on an overstuffed, wine-colored couch. Ruby pulled her feet up underneath her and began to enlighten Zoe. Ruby shared how when she was a senior in high school, she had secretly saved money for college by tutoring and entering (and winning) dance contests because her parents wanted her to get married after high school and wouldn't even consider paying for her to go to college. But eventually, they realized she was determined, and her dad did end up paying for her schooling. She went on to tell Zoe how she finally made her way up to Chicago after finishing business college and trying to work in Oilton. Zoe was shocked that Ruby had kept it quiet for so long.

"I just wanted a fresh start, you know?" Ruby explained.

"I can relate," Zoe said.

The clock struck one while Ruby was pouring the second cup of tea.

"If you liked Arthur enough to go out with him, even though you weren't going to marry him, why didn't you want to go out on dates with men here, or at least dance with them?" asked Zoe.

"Well, that is another long story," said Ruby. "Let's just say I wanted to focus on becoming exceptional at my job. I was entering a man's world, and there was no time for romance. I wanted men to know I meant business."

"I can respect that," Zoe said. "But what has changed? Why are you open to having a man in your life now?"

"Oh, I don't know." Ruby paused. "I can't really explain it. Something came over me tonight, and I just let loose."

"Well, that you did!" Zoe agreed and laughed.

Ruby chuckled and then the two girls broke out laughing. When the laughter finally petered out, Zoe cleared her throat.

"Now I have a bit of news for you. The clarinet player approached me while you were in the powder room and asked about you. I told him you don't give out your information, but he insisted." She raised her eyebrows and continued. "So don't be surprised if a guy named Edward shows up out of nowhere."

"What!" Ruby sat up straight. "Why would you do that?"

"Oh, don't worry," Zoe said. "He said he is not in town that much, so he probably never will, but you never know." Zoe picked up her purse and headed for the door. "Besides, I thought it would be good for you to have a male friend."

Ruby started to protest, but Zoe held her hand up, stopping her in her tracks. Then she smiled and bid Ruby good night, closing the door behind her.

Ruby stood staring at the door in shock. "Oh, my, how am I supposed to sleep now!" she mumbled to herself. "The clarinet man asked about me?"

She walked over to her desk and pulled out her journal, hoping that writing would help her calm down.

It is hard to believe it's 1928, and I have a college degree. I am a businesswoman making a difference in the world. Just like I set out to do. So, I think this year, I will make it a point to put music back in my life. I feel so alive. On that note, good night!

The following day was frosty, so Ruby bundled up as usual for work and headed to her streetcar stop to make her way to The Fair, the impressive eleven-story department store where she now worked. She had to keep telling herself that to really believe it! Ruby was proud to write home to her parents and let them know she landed a job as an accountant at such a prestigious store, which took up four blocks— State, Adams, Marble, and Dearborn— of the main shopping area in downtown Chicago. It was easy to get to work because all the streetcars made their way to that area. The Fair Store was known worldwide because of its size and motto: "Everything for everybody under one roof."

Ruby enjoyed arriving at work once the store was already opened and bustling with activity. She worked from nine thirty to five thirty and made it a point to enter from Adams Street so she could walk by the assortment of fine jewelry and, if there was time, take a peek. If Ruby arrived early enough, she would go to the ladies' section to look at gloves, handkerchiefs, and gorgeous silk and velvet dresses.

When it was time for work, Ruby would take the elevator up to the tenth floor, where the offices were, and join the other accountants there. Ruby had proven herself, demonstrating her bookkeeping knowledge, and earned the privilege of sitting at a desk at the front of the accounting department.

Ruby was not the first woman to work for The Fair as a bookkeeper; more women were graduating with relevant skills. When companies moved men up to management positions, they hired women as bookkeepers, but still for a lower wage. Ruby enjoyed her job and came to know Marsha, who had worked for The Fair for about a year. Marsha trained Ruby, but the relationship did not extend outside of the workplace. Marsha was busy with her love life, and her siblings and parents lived nearby. It was a great working relationship with mutual respect.

The real work drama Ruby would hear about always came from a few of the salesclerks in the glove department. Ruby enjoyed wearing gloves, not just to keep her hands warm in winter but to complete any outfit. If she could have them in every color, she would. Men were generally aware of how much women enjoyed their gloves and would purchase them for their lady friends, or as one clerk would say, "the other women." The saleswomen would start rattling off gossip even though nobody asked. Ruby found the information amusing, something to break the monotony of numbers in her head. But her ears perked up when she heard Mr. John Wiess's name. Rumor was that he was to be married. Ruby's face turned white, and she faltered.

"Are you all right?" asked the gossiping salesgirl.

Ruby nodded, and the salesgirl continued talking about how Mr. Wiess had bought the most expensive gloves for his fiancée. "She is from a well-to-do family here in Chicago, you know." She leaned closer. "Well, Ruby, that sale made me a week's worth of commissions all by itself."

She rattled on, but Ruby wasn't listening anymore because her stomach was becoming more upset.

"Are you sure you are all right?" the salesgirl asked again.

"Oh, yes," she stammered. "Th-thanks for the entertainment; time to go crunch numbers."

In reality, Ruby had a little more time for her lunch break, but she couldn't listen anymore and made her way to the powder room. She took a paper towel, ran it under the tap, and wiped her face. As Ruby looked in the mirror, she was surprised she had

had such a reaction to the news. *I decided to end it. Silly me to be reacting this way,* she thought to herself. She reached for a folded towel and dried her hands and face. Ruby opened her purse and powdered her face but did not need to pinch her already flushed cheeks.

The rest of the day, Ruby tried hard not to think of the news and went about her daily work.

On the way home, she let her mind focus on other matters, trying not to think about what could have been, but by bedtime, she was reliving a moment in time.

Shortly after she had left the insurance company, she had run into her old boss at the café where they first met. He was pleased to learn she had moved to her own place and invited Ruby to join him for dinner, and that is when their whirlwind romance had begun.

John and Ruby seemed to be inseparable from that night on. Ruby loved attending galas and political functions with John. He spoiled her with beautiful gowns, dressed her like a princess, and never once took

advantage of her. That is not to say they did
not have romantic candlelit dinners. Some
dinners took place at John's home and would
turn into heated moments of passion, but
Ruby always knew how to stop and make
him take her home before they went too far.
Ruby did not want to go all the way without
a wedding ring, but John told her he loved
the challenge. Ruby shared stories of her
steamy weekends spent with John with her
close friends, and they all agreed they loved
a man who respected boundaries.

Some weekends, John would help Ruby
in the food kitchens feeding the poor. He
loved how she was always collecting coats
and warm clothes to give to those who
could not afford them and how involved she
was in some of the guilds in her church. He
enjoyed that Ruby was always reading and
keeping up with politics, and they would
have heated debates on social issues. He
shared his business opportunities with Ruby,
and she never had a problem letting him
know if something was bothering her. John
said he liked that about her. He knew she
wanted him for him and not his money. They
had mutual respect and believed in many
of the same social issues, like women's
paychecks—not everyone thought like John

that women should have equal pay. However,
they differed on one important issue. One
night she found out that he felt that once
a woman married, she should stay home and
raise the children. Ruby thought you could
do both. She recalled how it could ruin a
night if they got on to that subject.

Ruby took a deep breath and gazed out
the window, remembering that horrible night
when it all fell apart.

Just when Ruby thought she would give
her heart entirely to John, the truth was
revealed. A tear rolled down her face as she
relived the moment. John had taken Ruby
out the week before and had her select a
gown for a charity fundraiser. Ruby was
excited, as it was taking place at the famous
Drake Hotel. When Ruby was at Chillicothe
College, she and her friends had read about
such high society parties and dreamed about
what it would be like to go to a dance there,
and now she was. Ruby could not wait to
write Clara a letter and tell her all about it.
It was like a fairy tale, and she thought this
would be the night John would ask her to
marry him. Ruby could not believe how lucky
she was to win the heart of a handsome,
kind, politically minded man who knew how to

treat a lady. How fortunate she had been to come to Chicago.

The fundraiser was a lovely event. Ruby's gown was a beautiful emerald green and a classic style that would remain ageless. John placed a beautiful pearl necklace around her neck and said it was a strand of pearls for a lovely lady. Ruby was the belle of the ball and was having a fantastic night.

John bid on a train trip to California for two, and Ruby hoped it would be for their honeymoon. Her mind wandered, thinking of all that would most likely happen. They danced the night away, and the slow dances could not have been more romantic.

After the last slow dance, they returned to their table and enjoyed a quiet moment together, and Ruby thought this might be the time she had anticipated and built up in her mind even though she did not know for sure. She was just hoping in the way girls do. Then a drunk Walter came over to their table and sat down.

"So, John, is this the girl you have been talking to us about?" He slurred and leered. "Hi, I am Walter, but you can call me Wally."

"Yes, Walter, it is," John said quickly.

"Now that you've met, you can go back where you came from."

"Not so fast; you never told us Ruby was so beautiful. Had your brother Masons known, we would have helped you." Walter wiped his chin with the back of his wrist. "You can call me Wally," he slurred again.

"What do you mean, 'brother Masons'?" Ruby asked.

"Walter, you can leave now." John stood up and started to pull Walter to his feet.

"No, John, I want to know what he is talking about." Ruby crossed her arms.

"Oh, you don't know!" Wally pulled his shoulder from John's grip. "Ah, John, have you kept it a secret from her, all this time? Shame on you."

"You need to shut up, Walter," John said through gritted teeth.

"No, Walter, tell me." Ruby glared at John.

"Well, if you insist . . . John is a Freemason like James, your dad."

"How do you know my dad's name?" Ruby asked.

"We all do." Walter shrugged. "John was asked to watch over you when you landed in Chicago."

Ruby swung toward John. "Is that true?"

"Yes, but I can explain!"

"Oh dear, I guess I let the cat out of the bag." Walter stood up and stumbled out of John's reach. "I think I better go now."

"Yes, you better." John threw Walter's coat at him. "I will deal with you later."

He turned and followed Ruby. "Ruby, let me explain," he called after her.

"There is nothing to explain," she said over her shoulder. "I am going home."

He caught up and spun her around. "Look, Ruby, please . . . can we just talk?"

Ruby stopped, realizing she was making a scene, and lowered her voice. "Fine, but over there, away from everyone."

John led her to an alcove and began to explain.

"Look, your dad contacted our chapter and just wanted to be sure you were OK. You should be grateful your dad cares about you that much." John ran his hand through his hair. "After all, Chicago, or any city for that matter, can be dangerous for a single, good-looking woman. So, I volunteered."

Ruby gave him a stern look and raised an eyebrow. "So, I never really earned the job on my own, is that what you are saying?"

"No . . . well, yes . . . I mean, no." John shook his head. "Look. I needed an operator.

You just happened to be close by, and I figured I would check you out. I figured you'd find a different job, and I would make sure you were safe. Then it turned out you learned quickly, and I decided you would make a good employee. Then, I found out you're qualified to work in accounting. It seemed like a win-win." He rushed to finish.

"A win-win? Yes, I was qualified and did a superior job for you." Ruby sighed.

"Yes, you did, and I never once took advantage of you. Look, Ruby, everything that has happened over these last few months has been real." His tone softened "My feelings for you are real."

"John, answer me this. How long have you and my dad been communicating?"

He took a deep breath before he answered. "Eight years."

"So, you know my dad and consider yourself to be one of his brothers, is that right?" Ruby's eyes bored into his. "Never mind, I already know the answer. Take me home, please."

They left the party, and John flagged his driver to pick them up. They rode home in total silence. Then, just as they were about to pull up to her residence, Ruby took off

the necklace he had given her and handed it
to him.

"Thank you for the beautiful gift, but I
can't keep it. I want to return it so I won't
ever be reminded of you. You do not need to
see me to the door. Thank you, Mr. Wiess,
and goodbye," Ruby said as she got out of
the car. She thanked the driver and wished
him well.

John got out of the car too. "But Ruby, I
have an important question for you."

"John, I had hoped you did as well. I did,
but this changes everything."

"Ruby, you can't let something like this
come between us," John said.

"Yes, I can. Good night, John." She
walked away.

Ruby had tears in her eyes as she opened
the door to the main entrance and took the
elevator up to her apartment. She would
never have dreamed the night would end the
way it did.

She did not see John again no matter how
many times he tried. John had come to her
office; he sent her flowers and waited for her
at her residence at the end of the day, but
ultimately, he realized it was over.

Ruby was grateful she was living in a
place where men were not allowed up to the

apartments; if allowed, she felt John would have camped outside her door. If that had happened, she probably would have given in to him.

One day, Doug and Liz were in town, and Liz and Ruby had time to catch up. Ruby shared with Liz what had happened with John.

"You're unbelievable," Liz said. "You let your red-headed stubbornness get in the way of being with someone who loves you."

Ruby wasn't swayed, but no matter how often she tried to interject, Liz would have none of it. Liz even tried to get Ruby to call John and arrange for the four of them to have dinner and catch up; this would give Ruby her opportunity to make up with John.

"Liz, it's too late. John is engaged to be married."

Liz looked at her and shook her head. "Well, then it was not meant to be."

Liz stayed for about a half-hour longer, and the girls then parted ways. They both agreed to stay in touch and hugged each other as Doug arrived to pick Liz up.

Ruby closed the door, but the conversation made her wonder once more . . .

what if? *What if I had accepted his flowers and apology? Would I be married now?* Then Ruby remembered the most crucial thing—John did not believe in a woman working once married, and he had hidden from her the truth that their meeting was a setup. That cleared Ruby's brain of the romance fog and brought her back to reality. She looked up to the sky and gave thanks. She was strong enough to stand on her own and reach for the stars. She continued to look out the window, gazing at the stars, and remembered her momma's words. "Ruby, only time will tell if you made the right choice, but as my momma always said, 'Life is choices, and you have to live with them!'" *I know I made the right choice. May John be happy, and on to the next chapter of life. Hmmm . . . I wonder if that clarinet player will call?*

A MONTH FILLED WITH SURPRISES

FEBRUARY 1928

The arctic February wind was picking up as Ruby went back to volunteering at Grace United Methodist to help collect coats for the poor. Ruby entered the church hall, where parishioners held large meetings, bazaars, and meals. She was excited to bring in three children's coats that a salesgirl from work had donated to the cause. Though it wasn't snowing in Chicago, Ruby felt the bitter wind made it colder than she thought possible. Nevertheless, helping with the church outreach program for the poor was a cause that was important to her. She was surprised when she walked in to find table after table set up with around fifty boxes of coats.

The head of the outreach program, Mildred, was pleased to show everyone all the new donations that had come in over the past few weeks. She explained how each table was set up according to size, age, and gender. There were tables for men, women, boys, girls, and infants.

Ruby noted that blankets had also come in, which parishioners had already cleaned and had ready to go to some of the settlement houses.

About ten women of various ages showed up, and the sorting began. It took several hours, but no one seemed to mind. Ruby came to learn more about what her fellow parishioners from all walks of life did to help the poor and newly arrived immigrants. One church member explained with pride how Chicago attracted people from all over the world, like Italians, Poles, Swedes, Germans, Greeks, Czechs, and Irish, to name a few. Ruby was happy to help people regardless of where they were from. Her momma had taught Ruby and her siblings that when God blessed them with something, no matter how little or big, they needed to turn around and help others. That is what the world was about—being kind to one another. Ruby knew helping people stay warm was a wonderful way to give back, especially in the winter. Ruby once told a parishioner how keeping warm was especially important to her, as when she first arrived in Chicago, friends helped her prepare for a cold she had never imagined. She told them how her fingertips and toes would turn so blue, and it would take hours to warm them up with the help of gloves and boots.

A few hours later, the boxes were refilled and labeled. Several men picked up the boxes and delivered them to the families who needed them most. Ruby had seen the men before, but there was a new guy in town that caught her eye. Ruby went to pick up a lighter box to take to the man, but he quickly rushed over and took it from her and struck up a conversation; it was exactly what Ruby had hoped he would do.

His name was Ralph, and he had a smile that would warm even the coldest heart.

The women watched Ruby and Ralph's interaction, and one woman came over and

asked Ruby to help her with another box.
Ralph put the box in the truck and returned
for more; this time, he slipped a note
to Ruby.

How can I contact you?

Ruby acted like she had not received the
message and kept a poker face. She waited
a few minutes and went to the ladies' room,
where she wrote on the back of his note:

*I do not give out my information, but
I am happy to meet you after work
tomorrow. There is a coffee shop
across from The Fair. I will meet you
at 5:15. Give me a nod if that works
for you.*

Ruby handed Ralph another box, and later
when he returned from placing the box on the
truck, he nodded yes to her, and she nodded
back without a smile so as not to give away
to the other women what was going on.
The truck was filled and ready for
delivery. The women began cleaning up;
the men would put the tables away and do
the last bit of tidying up. Mildred thanked
everyone, and they all felt good about their

accomplishments. Mildred reminded them they
would continue collecting coats, boots, and
blankets and meet again in two weeks.

Ruby caught the streetcar back to her
place, happy to be out of the wind and
excited about meeting Ralph the next day.

Ruby could hardly concentrate at work and,
at the end of the day, headed to the coffee
shop as quickly as possible. She arrived
early and was lucky enough to get a table
where they could chat and hopefully not be
disturbed by other patrons. Ruby faced the
window so she could see when Ralph arrived
and wave at him. It occurred to her that she
was about to meet a member of the opposite
sex and did not even know his last name.
Now she was worried she might be stood
up. At the same time, she did not want to
seem overly anxious, so she got out a book,
pretending it did not matter whether he
showed up or not.

Ruby became so interested in her book
she almost missed seeing Ralph come in.
It worked to her advantage, as it truly
did seem she was not eagerly awaiting
his arrival.

Ralph walked up to the table and greeted
Ruby and thanked her for meeting him. The
waitress came, and they each ordered a
coffee. Ralph offered to order her a bite to
eat, but Ruby said she was not hungry for
dinner yet, maybe a light snack. Ruby did
not want to tell him the real reason—that
she didn't want to waste his time or money
eating if in ten minutes they decided to part
company and go about their business.

Ralph looked at Ruby, and a light seemed
to dawn as he caught her drift. "Well, it is
the dinner hour."

Ruby smiled and said, "Well then, let's
spoil our dinner and share a slice of their
cherry pie."

As they sat there talking and enjoying
the warm pie, Ruby learned he was Ralph
Garland, and he worked over at Ford Motor
Company overseeing the production line.
He shared with Ruby how the assembly line
worked, and because of it, Ford was able
to manufacture many cars. Ruby could tell
Ralph was very proud of the work he did. The
two went back and forth, sharing the typical
small talk. In the end, Ralph gave Ruby a
lift home in his car, and they agreed to have
dinner the following Saturday. He walked
Ruby to her door and said he would pick her

up at five o'clock since Ruby had said she
wanted an early dinner.

With that, they bid each other good night.
Ruby went straight to Zoe's room to tell her
what had happened, but she was not in. Ruby
went to her room and closed the door, quite
pleased with how the meeting with Ralph
had gone. She found she was looking forward
to Saturday.

Ruby thought Saturday would never come.
She was excited to have dinner with Ralph.
They had not spoken during the week.
Living in the Eleanor Club made it difficult,
as there was just one phone for the one
hundred girls living there, and there was zero
privacy. The phone was located in a private
booth, but women lined up to make a call
and would pound on the door if a girl took
too long. For the most part, the girls were
polite enough that if a guy did call one of
the girls and she was not there to pick up,
someone would run and get her. Polite young
ladies did not call gentlemen, and so it was
mutually beneficial for the girls to help each
other out when a gentleman called. There
was an understanding, an unwritten rule, that

if you arranged to have a gentleman call you, you should be by the phone when he did call. Girls would even leave notes if they were expecting a call at a specific time. It was an effective system, but it did mean people knew your business.

Ruby preferred not to be the subject of idle gossip. So, when Ralph showed up one night to take her out, she knew it would give the house mother, Mrs. Smith, and any other girls close by plenty to talk about once she left the building.

Ruby noticed how Ralph looked at her when she greeted him in the waiting area. She smiled to herself as she took his arm and they walked to the car.

"Ruby, if it were not impolite to whistle at a lady, I would give a huge whistle," said Ralph. "Let me just say, you are the cat's meow!"

Ruby smiled at Ralph as she got in the car. He closed her door and quickly hopped in the driver's seat. Ruby was wearing a beautiful flower print scarf that she had purchased to accessorize her long-waisted, navy-blue dress with pleats. In addition, she had on a fashionable hat that seemed to fit all occasions. Ralph was taking Ruby to The Village, an Italian restaurant that she

had heard great things about but had never
been to.

When the couple entered the restaurant,
they were shown to a booth, and Ruby took
in her surroundings. She wanted to absorb
every detail, as she felt like she had stepped
into a village in Italy.

"Do you like it?" Ralph asked, obviously
eager to please her.

"Oh, yes, it's so lovely," Ruby replied.
"The white tablecloths, the beautiful silver,
the cherrywood chairs, the red booth . . .
it's all so beautiful, right down to the small
flower vases on each table." She sighed.
"Who would not be happy?"

The waiter set down two glasses of water
and asked if they would be interested in
something else to drink before dinner and
handed them the menu. They each ordered
iced tea and continued reading the menu.

"Please, order whatever you're in the
mood for," Ralph told Ruby.

They each decided to order something
different so they could sample a variety of
foods. Ruby ordered the fettucine alfredo
while Ralph dove into a cannelloni.

For dessert, they chose a *Torta Barozzi*,
an Italian chocolate cake, and they
discovered they both loved chocolate.

After dinner, Ralph paid the check, and the two left and went for an evening drive along Lake Shore Drive near the Drake Hotel. It was too windy and cold to go for a walk, but bundled up and snuggled close, they enjoyed the drive and getting to know each other better. They discovered they enjoyed talkies, so they agreed to see a picture show on their next date.

When Ralph pulled up in front of Ruby's place, she leaned over and gave him a quick peck on the cheek.

"The ladies will be watching at the door," she explained.

"Understood." Ralph gave a nod and grinned, waving toward the house. "I'm just happy we had such a great evening and you enjoyed the restaurant."

He went around to her side of the car and opened the door, then walked her to her front door. He reached for her hand, brought it up to his mouth, and kissed it.

"Good night, Ralph, I had a lovely night," Ruby said as she pulled her hand away. She opened the door, walked in, and closed it behind her, leaving Ralph standing on the stoop.

"Welcome home," said Mrs. Smith. "So,

the lucky fellow did not earn his way into the sitting room?"

"Maybe next time," Ruby replied. She excused herself as she headed to her room.

Ruby enjoyed living at the Eleanor Club and did not mind Mrs. Smith watching out for the girls, but since it was her first time having a gentlemen caller, Ruby did not know how to respond and only hoped she was not too impolite with her clipped reply.

Chapter 11

WHAT JUST HAPPENED?

MAY— JULY 1928

By May, Ralph and Ruby had become an item, and when they were not working, they were joined at the hip. Ruby told her momma and Zoe that she could not have been happier. The two lovebirds spent most of their free time at church functions, especially doing charity work. Ruby and Ralph enjoyed serving food to the needy on Saturdays. It seemed more and more people were out of work and going hungry, and they counted on the church for help.

The church vestry had also noticed the uptick in need, so they began serving food after the last service on Sundays as well. Ruby and Ralph would have a bite to eat

at the church and help serve the hungry on
Sundays too. They discussed the news of
the day—of job losses and the stock market
fluctuating—and hoped it would get better
for everyone.

Despite everything that was going on,
there were still good things happening;
the world seemed to be opening up with
possibilities. For Ruby and Ralph, listening to
jazz music—and for Ruby, women getting the
vote—made it a great time to be alive.

The month flew by, and one Sunday in
June, after serving at the church, the two
were getting in the car. As Ralph opened the
door for Ruby, he looked at her and paused.

"You know, Ruby, what you said the other
day . . ." he began. "Well, you are right
about us being born at the perfect time." He
helped her into the car. "I just have to add
one little thing—my life is even better with
you in it."

Ruby smiled at him as he closed her
door. When he got in, she kissed him on
the cheek and said she was glad he was in
her life too. They both just smiled at one
another. It wouldn't have been proper to
have a romantic kiss in a church parking
lot. They had a relaxing drive back to
Ruby's place, and she invited Ralph into the

parlor. He needed to get home to prepare for the next day's work, so he declined her invitation. They agreed to see each other the following Saturday.

One night in July, Zoe and Ruby managed to spend a whole evening catching up on each other's lives. Ruby shared with Zoe how Ralph always told her he appreciated her financial sense, while she let Ralph talk about how the factory line worked and the pride the men took when the car rolled off, ready to sell.

"OK, as much as I love to hear all the dreary details of Ralph's work, I want to know the good stuff!" Zoe leaned in. "Do you even find a place to be alone? How does he kiss? Details please!"

"Zoe, I'm a lady, and I don't tell tales." Ruby giggled. "Honestly, kissing is all I really need. And Ralph respects me for that and seems fine with it."

There was definitely electricity, Ruby explained, but she had made it very clear to Ralph that she never wanted to be a "shotgun bride." Ralph respected her for

that, and they enjoyed going out with
one another.

At work, Ruby and the other bookkeepers
noticed that consumer spending was still in
the doldrums. The accountants had noted
it as early as 1927, and a year later, it
had not gotten any better; in fact, in some
departments, it was worse. The store tried
to improve things by having more items on
sale in the hopes of moving inventory.

One day the head accountant met with
the owner of the store and the managers of
the departments to share some bad news.
That evening Ruby told Ralph that the store
had to let more people go. Ralph shared
with Ruby how similar things were happening
at the factory, but according to the news,
things would turn around soon.

It was a mid-July, and Ralph and Ruby met
at around ten in the morning for a stroll
around Lincoln Park before the heat became
totally unbearable. Ralph had told Ruby
he had something to ask her, which made

her excited to see him. She was dressed in a pretty white lace dress and hat she had purchased for Easter. She did not think in any way he was going to pop the question, but she was eager to hear what he had on his mind.

Finally, after a bit of a stroll, they sat down to feed the squirrels with nuts Ralph had bought from a street vendor.

"You know, Ruby," he began as he threw nuts to the squirrels, "I've been thinking a lot about us lately and . . . well, you should know what I've been mulling over in my mind for some time."

Ruby was beginning to get butterflies from the suspense and found she was holding her breath.

Ralph stopped feeding the squirrels, took her hands, looked at her, and said, "Ruby, I decided I want to go to seminary school. I want to be a minister. The Divinity School at Duke University in Durham, North Carolina, has accepted me for this fall. Ruby, I want you to be my girl, and when I graduate, we can be a team helping others. You will make the perfect minister's wife. What do you think?"

Ruby was in shock as she looked at his beautiful blue eyes that would make any girl's heart stop. It was a lot to take in. Ruby sat quietly for a moment, gathering her thoughts, then looked at him.

"Ralph, I am so glad you have been called to be a minister. I can see you helping others and sharing your passion for the Lord." She paused and took a deep breath. "I do love the Lord, but I am in no way meant to be a minister's wife. I am too selfish."

Ralph looked crestfallen. He tried to convince Ruby she was meant to be a minister's wife, and that she could still work and use her skills to help with the economic part of running a church when the time was right. The more he talked, the bigger a hole he dug, convincing Ruby that never in a blue moon would she go down that path.

They rode silently home, and Ralph walked her to the door. They said goodbye, and Ruby wished him the best.

When Zoe checked in on Ruby after the date she had been so excited about, it was only to find her crying her heart out. Zoe was in shock just as much as Ruby.

"Did you not see the signs that he was thinking of becoming a minister? Did he not mention it even once?" Zoe asked over and over again.

Ruby shook her head no each time.

"What is wrong with me?" Ruby wailed. "Why do I keep attracting guys that can never be 'the one'?" Ruby blew her nose into her handkerchief. "If I did marry Ralph, my parents would be over the moon." She pouted. "They would be so proud to have a minister in the family."

But she could not do that, and Zoe understood. Ruby said she did not mean to be selfish, but she had worked so hard to be a businesswoman, and she wanted to move up in her job. To be a minister's wife, which was an incredible job, she would have to be willing to help others much more than her time would permit. Plus, to be the best minister's wife, she would want to be able to step up whenever he felt the congregation needed her.

"Besides, it will take him years to get his divinity degree," Ruby said. "And I am not sure I want to wait that long to get married."

The girls laughed.

"As if we want to walk down the aisle any time soon!" added Zoe. "I just want to stay home and eat Eskimo Pies all week."

Zoe rolled over and got serious. "Look, why don't we do something fun next weekend?" she suggested. "Let me see what's going on, maybe a baseball game, a movie, or even dancing. How does that sound?"

"OK, but no dancing. I am not in the mood to dance." Ruby sighed. "You know, we could just stay home, and I can get more ice cream, and we could just eat and be bored together."

"Nonsense." Zoe stood up with her hands on her hips. "Now you get some sleep, and I will be in touch with you during the week." She blew her a kiss and left, closing the door behind her.

Ruby smiled. She was so lucky to have a friend like Zoe. Who needed a silly ole man anyway?

The week seemed to pass slowly for Ruby as she robotically got dressed, went to work, came home, and went to bed. Zoe checked in on her and commented that Ruby was not her tidy self.

"I'm not in the mood to go out, Zoe," Ruby said. "I'm sorry."

"Don't give it another thought," said

Zoe. "We'll just stay in and do our nails and gossip this weekend. Just us girls. It'll be fun!"

Ruby rolled her eyes but gave in to her friend's enthusiastic suggestion, and the two chatted well into the wee hours.

By mid-August Ruby had hoped she would hear from Ralph, but not a word. He was not even at church. Ruby was helping at the church, boxing donated clothes, when she saw one of Ralph's friends, Mike, collecting the boxes and loading them into a truck to distribute. Mike told Ruby that Ralph had started going to a different church so he would not make her feel uncomfortable. She thanked him and asked him to tell Ralph that she sent her best. Mike told her that he would, but it really was best not to be exchanging messages. He told her Ralph needed to move on. Ruby's face turned white as she muttered in agreement and thanked him again. He nodded and went about his business loading the boxes.

That evening Zoe brought sandwiches, and Ruby shared that she had hurt Ralph deeper than she had imagined. Zoe listened as Ruby went on and on about how she had missed the signs—and how she had not known he was in love with her.

"I really thought we were just in the beginning stages of building a relationship," she said.

"Well, Ruby, it's been weeks, and it is high time to make a fresh start." Zoe was always good at turning things around to a positive. "You have to start getting out again." Ruby started to protest, and Zoe stopped her. "I mean to more than just church activities." She folded her arms across her chest. "I don't want to hear any ifs, ands, or buts. I am going to arrange something fun for the weekend . . . and no gentlemen," she finished and tipped her chin.

At the end of the workweek, Ruby was ecstatic to get home and out of the heat to relax. She loved it when she could get home, take off her brassiere, and just have on her gown and robe. She could not wait to find out what Zoe had planned for Saturday. All she knew was to go to Zoe's room at about four and dress casually.

At 4:00 p.m. sharp the following day, Ruby knocked on Zoe's door, and much to her surprise, Helen and Liz were there. Zoe had come to know Helen and Liz through Ruby, and they had all become friends. Ruby was overjoyed.

"We are having an all-nighter girls' night," Zoe said. "I told you no men, and so here we are, us girls, jazz music, and girl talk."

As the girls chattered on, catching up like old times, Helen shared how much she enjoyed her work at the university. She talked all about the exciting things going on, especially with the construction of the Home for Destitute and Crippled Children.

Liz shared how happy she was; this was the first time she had left her son, Jeffrey, overnight. "I admit, I'm nervous, but he is excited to be staying all night at Grandma's like a big boy." She stretched her arms over her head and sighed. "I was in need of a girls' night, and Doug said it was well deserved. I'm so lucky to have found a man that respects women enough to know they need time alone with girls just as much as their man time." She giggled.

Zoe had filled the girls in on Ruby and why she was down, but they were eager to hear Ruby's explanation of the situation.

Helen spoke up first. "Ruby, I must say, I'm surprised you let Ralph go," she began. "I could see you as a minister's wife."

"What? Why?" Ruby was so surprised.

Liz laughed. "Ruby, seriously? Listen . . . you don't 'fool around,' you don't drink, you don't smoke, you don't even say 'shoot.' You say 'crum' instead." The other girls started laughing too, and Liz continued. "When someone needs cheering up, who is there to help them? You are! You have a heart of gold."

Helen chimed in. "And where are you most weekends, during your time off? At church helping others. It only makes sense."

Ruby continued staring wide-eyed, her gaze moving from one girl to another. Everyone was quiet for a moment, waiting for her to reply.

Finally, Ruby said, "Oh my . . . well, I never looked at it like that." She sighed. "Before I came here, I thought everyone was like me. The only difference was that it was more acceptable in Chicago for women to work. I mean, obviously I knew there were fun times, but still, I thought only loose girls really let themselves go . . . and . . . you know . . ."

The other girls looked at each other, stifling more laughter.

"What?" asked Ruby.

Liz piped up. "Ruby, we just did not tell you."

"Oh? Tell me what?"

"Sorry, Ruby, while you were being holy, we were going to petting parties," she said, giggling. "And yes, some people went all the way." She looked at Helen and winked. "But I never did."

"I'm really not so holy." Ruby crossed her arms. "I've done some of that too." She was annoyed she hadn't been invited but now understood why the girls were so close.

"Look, Ruby," Zoe cut in, getting the conversation back on track. "The bottom line for you is the right person has not come along. You will know it when it happens. In the meantime, girls, let's put on some jazz. Lucky for you I am on the first floor, so we can dance and not disturb anyone below us."

The rest of the night was dancing, playing cards, eating, and of course, laughing.

The next day the girls woke up with sore backs from sleeping on the floor and couch. They enjoyed coffee and toast. They were very impressed with Zoe's Toastmaster. Zoe said her parents had given it to her for Christmas, and it saved her a lot of time.

The girls helped Zoe tidy up the apartment and then promised each other to write. Liz insisted they come to the farm for a weekend. The girls hugged each other goodbye, and Zoe closed the door and looked at Ruby, very pleased with herself.

"That is what I call a perfect weekend!" said Zoe.

"Thank you." Ruby smiled. "I am going to be just fine. Seriously though, petting parties? I would have never guessed. Do you go to those . . . never mind, I don't want to know."

Ruby gave her friend a hug and left to go back to her own room.

Chapter 12

THE PHONE CALL

Ruby spent the rest of summer focused on work and volunteering at the church. She even volunteered to help with the organ music during services when the organist was ill, which did not happen often. When Ruby was not volunteering or working, she was happy to spend the hot days indoors, reading and enjoying the peace and quiet. She set up a little reading area where she had a comfortable overstuffed chair with a tall lamp on one side and on the other side a table that her electric fan sat on to keep her cool.

Ruby was reading *The Hotel* by Elizabeth Bowen when the phone rang. In an instant,

her world turned upside down. Ruby hung up
the phone then immediately called her boss
and was given permission to go home. Later
that day, Ruby was boarding the first of two
trains that would take her to the Oklahoma
City train station, where her dad would pick
her up.

On the train ride back home, Ruby sat
thinking, *What a way to start September*,
and wondering how on earth her brother
Zach ended up in a car accident. With tears
rolling down her face as she looked out the
window, watching the countryside go by, she
prayed he would wake up and be **OK**.

Zach had been promoted to supervisor at
the Cushing-Drumright Oil Field, so he had
moved his family there to be closer to work.
Zach had developed a solid reputation for
work ethics and respect among the men he
managed. He was even known for smelling
the ground and would say to his boss, "I
can smell the oil." Whether he really could,
he was still known for being right. "No one
dug in a place just because," he said. It had
become a wager among his buddies. Ruby
smiled, recalling her brother telling her one

time on the phone, "I can smell it, and the men believe me."

Ruby could not understand how he would have been in a car accident on his drive home. When her dad picked her up from the train station, he filled her in on the rest of the story as they made their way to St. Anthony Hospital in Oklahoma City. He explained how it was the closest hospital to the accident even though it was quite a drive from Seminole.

It turned out that Zach had been asked by his boss to go and help in Seminole; the manager had taken ill, and Zach was to fill in until they received a replacement. It was a busy time. The Seminole oil boom brought jobs, towns grew, and eventually, 1,300 square miles in east-central Oklahoma had sixty petroleum reservoirs.

The accident happened one evening when Zach was exhausted from working extra-long shifts. The roads in some areas were not wide enough for two cars to pass comfortably. All Ruby's dad knew was from the other driver. Zach had been coming from the other direction, and it looked like he had seen the other driver coming and did not slow down enough for the curve. Zach went off the road, the car flipped, and Zach was thrown from the vehicle. Zach was unconscious on the way to the hospital and had not yet woken up when James left to pick her up from the train station.

When Ruby and her dad arrived at the hospital, Ruby's siblings were there, along with Zach's wife, Clara, and Ruby's momma, Zola. Ruby hugged her momma and turned to Clara, one of her best friends from college. Clara and Zach had met when he had come to visit Ruby in Chillicothe. Afterward, Clara had moved to New York and she and Zach had kept in touch, and finally Clara had given in to his charms and moved to Oklahoma.

Ruby hugged her friend, and they all sat down, waiting to hear when they could see Zach. The doctor was in the room with him, so no one could go in. Since it was critical care, only one person was allowed in at a time. Ruby sat quietly next to Clara, holding her hand.

Finally, Clara spoke. "Do you ever think about our days in Chillicothe?"

Ruby nodded yes, knowing that Clara just needed to keep her mind off things.

Clara kept talking. "Isn't it funny? I mean, the whole thing with you wanting to go to college, your brother looking for you, I met him . . ." Her voice stuck in her throat. "And now look, we are married. I never thanked you for your shenanigans. I never would have met Zach if you had not dared to do what you did." Tears rolled down her cheeks. "Ruby, he is the love of my life. I don't know what I would do without him."

Ruby was about to respond when the doctor walked over to the family. Clara jumped up, hoping for good news.

"Please come with me, Mrs. Dinsmore." The doctor motioned for Clara to follow him.

The rest of the family stood quietly, each fighting with their own thoughts, wondering what was going on, as they watched Clara and the doctor walk into Zach's room. Ruby's parents were beside themselves. It was the first time Ruby had ever seen them not in charge of their children. Ruby watched her mom sink into her dad's arms, and for the first time in Ruby's life, she saw her momma looking old and helpless.

James guided Zola to a chair, and Rilla came and sat next to her parents and took her momma's hands. The rest of the family surrounded Ruby's parents, and Ruby watched them. She wanted to join them but first took in the closeness they each had for one another. A maturity had come into the

family that Ruby had missed out on by living
so far away. Ruby had pictured everyone the
way they were, but now she saw that just
as she had grown up, so had they. She felt
like an outsider in her own family, but she
knew from their earlier greeting that she was
not. Yet, she could not help but feel that
way. Ruby joined the family circle around her
parents, and they began to pray.

Clara walked up just as they finished the
prayer led by her dad, and all eyes turned
toward her. She made her way to Zola, who
stood up, and Clara took her hands.

"OK, this is what we know so far." She
inhaled deeply. "The doctor wanted to
share with me that they have hope. Even
though Zach is unconscious, he responded
when they asked him to move a finger if he
could hear them. He did try lifting his hand,
and the doctors say that is a good sign."
She paused to collect her thoughts. "They
thought Zach might open his eyes if he heard
my voice, but he did not. They are hoping
it is just a matter of time. The doctor says
that often when a patient moves their hand,
they are trying to wake up, so we have to
be patient."

Clara turned to Ruby. "Why don't you go

in and see him. Your voice might be what he needs to hear."

Ruby and her dad walked down the hall, and Ruby looked at the door and pushed it open.

She saw her brother lying against stark white sheets, helpless, in a deep sleep. Ruby kissed him on the forehead and pulled a chair up next to his bed. She took his hand and started talking about all the fun times they had together as kids. She talked about him playing football in high school and how much the girls loved to decorate his locker. Ruby rambled on about many things, hoping something would wake him up, but nothing seemed to do the trick. She even reminded him how he and their dad went looking for her when they heard she ran off to college and how he was very upset about it. Zach lay there unresponsive. Ruby kissed his forehead again. It was time to let another sibling have some time with him. They were only allowed five minutes per visit, as the doctor said he needed to rest.

Clara slept all night in a waiting room chair, hoping Zach might wake up. Ruby had gone back home with James and Zola and had been up all night looking at her momma's book about herbal medicine. She spoke to her momma the following day about what she had read. Zola looked amazingly bright-eyed considering the situation.

"I agree, Ruby! I should have thought of my herbal remedies myself, but sometimes when a patient is your own family, your mind goes blank."

They went outside to her herb garden and picked some peppermint. James drove Ruby and Zola back to the hospital, where they found Clara. With Clara's permission, Zola went in to see Zach first. She wanted to try something but wanted Clara to know that if he did wake up, it would be because of her experiment. Zola did not want Clara to take it personally if he woke up for his momma and not for her.

Clara understood. Ruby was amazed at how close Momma and Clara had become. Her momma was very sensitive to Clara's feelings, which touched Ruby. Zola entered the room with peppermint leaves and peppermint hand lotion that she had grabbed right before they left the house. Zola held two peppermint leaves up to Zach's nose for him to inhale. Then she laid them on his upper lip. Zola took some of the lotion and rubbed it on his temples as she quietly prayed. She then went to Zach's feet and rubbed the lotion on his feet and toes. Next, she pressed gently on his ankles as she rubbed the cream into his skin. She then took his hands, did the same, and returned to the temples. Zach stirred a little, and as Zola massaged his head, she saw Clara at the door. Zola motioned for her to come in, took her hands, and showed her how to rub his head. Ruby was also watching from the door, taking in the scene, remembering her momma's medical skills that she had witnessed years ago when she had watched Zola deliver a baby. Zola held the peppermint leaves up to his nose one more time for a good sniff, took the leaf with her, and stepped out of the room, putting her arm around Ruby's shoulder as they both watched Clara from the hallway.

Clara kept rubbing and looking at Zola, and then Clara started singing "Amazing Grace" as she massaged his head. She leaned over and whispered in his ear. He opened his eyes.

Clara yelled, "The peppermint worked, he woke up!"

Excitement took over, and nurses and

doctors came running to the room. Zola and Ruby went to the waiting room to get James; the rest of the family was not there yet.

They waited for almost half an hour while the doctors examined him, but eventually the family was allowed in to see Zach.

Whatever Clara had whispered, that and the peppermint must have done the trick. The doctors needed to run some tests, so Clara came and joined the others as tears of joy ran down her face. Clara hugged Zola and thanked her for the peppermint.

"Actually, Ruby deserves all the credit," said Zola. "She stayed up all night looking for answers."

Clara hugged Ruby with all her might.

The family sat there till the doctors came with an update. They were going to move Zach to a standard room, as it looked like he would make a full recovery. However, they wanted to keep him for several more days to help him regain his strength and ensure no unexpected issues arose. The doctors marveled at how lucky Zach was to have been thrown far enough away from the car that it did not roll on him. He suffered a few broken ribs and a broken arm, and a nasty bump on his head that had caused the concussion.

The family was thrilled with the news. The next few days flew by, and before they knew it, Zach was going home. Before Ruby left to return to Chicago, everyone met at Zach's house. Clara had called and said there was some news. As they gathered in the family room, Zach was in a chair with Clara standing by his side. Everyone looked intensely at Zach, fearing the worst.

"Thank you for coming, everyone," Zach began. "I wanted to thank you for being at the hospital for me . . . and for Clara." He looked up at her and smiled. "Your love helped bring me back." He paused and looked at each member of the family, one at a time, as the intensity in the room grew. "The bonus to all this is what Clara whispered in my ear in the hospital. . . . Our family will be growing!"

Everyone looked at each other as the news sank in, and their expressions went from worry to excitement, then pure joy.

"I knew you must have said something miraculous." Zola clapped her hands together in prayer and looked up.

Clara nodded. Zola reached for her, pulled her close, and hugged her tight. "Bless you."

People did not stay much longer, as Zach still needed to rest. But the crisis was over, and a new life was coming, and the family was feeling very grateful.

That Sunday, Ruby attended church with her family, which was always a special time with her parents and any siblings who were still living at home. Ruby sat next to her mom and felt all warm inside as she softly sang so she could hear her mom's sweet voice singing "Rock of Ages."

Rilla and Gerald were back at the Dinsmore home preparing dinner for everyone for when they returned home from church. Everyone was delighted when they walked through the front door, as the aromas of Momma's fried chicken and stir-fried potatoes with onions swirled through the air. Rilla had even made a lemon pie for dessert.

After dinner, Zola went to lie down, and the boys headed to their smokehouse, while Rilla and Ruby cleaned up. As they were happily cleaning, Ruby mentioned to her sister that she would be making arrangements to head back to Chicago on the next available train. Rilla stopped washing dishes and stared at Ruby.

"What?" Ruby put down her tea towel and took a step back as Rilla glared at her.

"You do not want to know what I am thinking." Rilla turned to dry the plate she was holding and huffed.

"I do believe I know what you're thinking, *sister*. Rilla—"

"Enough, Ruby!"

Ruby was startled by her sister's stern voice.

"So, you have not been home in almost two years, and now we have you here but only because Zach almost died, and you can't even stay a few more days? You would do this to Momma?"

"Do *what* to Momma?" Ruby glared back at Rilla.

"Just how blind *are* you?" Rilla asked. "Can you not tell how happy Momma is to have you here? Can you not tell that Momma and Daddy are not spring chickens anymore? They need us, and you are not here to help!" Rilla threw the towel on the counter. "Momma misses you, and Lordy, I don't know why. It's not like you helped her with chores that much when you were living here!"

"Now, wait a minute!" Ruby said.

The sisters were at each other when their

dad came in for some water and saw them
quarreling like two schoolgirls.

"Now, girls, settle down." He came and
stood between them. "Your momma needs
rest and doesn't need to hear you bickering."
He took Ruby's tea towel and pretended
to swat them. "Now, go out back and get
some air and discuss your differences like
the young ladies we raised you to be, not a
couple of hooligans."

The girls went to the backyard and sat on
the wicker chairs in the garden.

"I'm sorry, Rilla," Ruby said. "I'm willing
to listen."

Rilla explained how even though their
momma did not need to cook as much now,
she still had two kids left at home, but
now there were grandkids to look after too.
She barely had time to check on patients
who wanted her to deliver their babies. She
was still the backup person for deliveries
in the town to free up the doctor for
other matters.

"Zach just got home, and now you want
to take off."

"Oh, Rilla, I know it doesn't seem right."
Ruby tried to explain her job commitments,
but Rilla wouldn't have it.

"It's high time you forgot about all that

foolishness and acted like a woman. Let the man's world be and come home."

"Rilla! I thought you understood and supported me. I'm really doing well and making a difference."

"Ruby, you always were a rebel," said Rilla. "You could not be happy like the rest of us, even when you had a beau who wanted to marry you. You broke his heart." Rilla crossed her arms and turned away. "Well, shame on you; you deserve to be alone. That's all I have to say. I have it out of my system."

"I'm sorry you feel that way," Ruby said quietly. "I thought you were proud of me and what I've accomplished."

"I am in some ways proud of you," Rilla replied. "But in other ways, you made some of us girls feel like you were better than us." She took Ruby's hand in hers. "The bottom line is if you could just forget about work long enough and stay at least until Zach is on his feet, it would please Momma, and it would be a big help to Clara. And besides, what if he takes a turn for the worse? You would have to come back. This way you are already here."

"I guess you're right," Ruby agreed. "I'll

call my boss in the morning and see what I can work out."

The two girls hugged and made up, and Rilla and Gerald left to make their way to their own home.

Zola told Ruby she was happy her girls had resolved their issues. Ruby was embarrassed that her momma had heard the ruckus and promised to do better.

The following day Ruby heard a knock at the front door and answered it. She did not recognize the woman standing there holding a plate of cookies; she introduced herself as Mrs. Woods.

"Arthur Woods's wife?" Ruby asked.

"Yes, that is correct. You must be Ruby," she replied. "Arthur told me you might be home. We heard about your brother's accident. I hope he's well." She paused and when Ruby didn't reply, she cleared her throat and continued. "I understand you two were together in high school." She smiled, putting Ruby slightly more at ease. "Thank you for not wanting him, because I'm one lucky girl."

Ruby finally found her voice and

remembered her manners. She took the plate of cookies. "Thank you for the cookies. Won't you come in?"

"Oh no, thank you though," she said. "I really need to get to the hardware store. Arthur is by himself." She took a step back to leave, then stopped. "He enjoys me being there. I must say, we do make the perfect working couple. I do the inventory and the books, and he does all the selling." She gave a tight-lipped smile and looked Ruby up and down.

Ruby politely thanked her once more as Mrs. Woods turned and headed down the walkway to her car.

Ruby put the cookies in the kitchen, mimicking Arthur's wife under her breath. "We make the perfect couple." Then, a bit louder, not sure who she was trying to convince, she said, "I did not break his heart! He understood from the beginning of our courtship that we each had plans to go to college—the nerve of her!" Ruby was still grumbling to herself when Ida Jane came in.

"Let it go, Ruby," she said. "People are going to think what they want. And you cannot do anything about it."

Ruby spun around and blushed. "When did

you get so smart?" she asked and hugged her
little sister.

"I don't know. I just did," Ida Jane
replied.

The sisters giggled and went into the
family room and plunked down on the couch
to catch up on the family and life in town.

A couple of days passed. Ruby's boss had
told her to take all the time she needed—but
not too long. Ruby did not know what that
meant, but she would play it by ear.

Zola loved having Ruby home, and Ruby
enjoyed helping her momma bake, which
surprised her momma very much. Ruby also
took full advantage of enjoying her favorite
reading spot and sat there in her alcove
at the top of the stairs, looking out the
window and recalling her youth. Before Ruby
came down for supper, she would glance at
herself in her momma's gold-framed mirror
and remember looking in it before going
downstairs to meet Arthur. There were many
memories in the family home, some of which
Ruby had not thought of in years. As she
glanced in the mirror this time, she said,
"Ruby, you are not the little girl you once

were. I hope you like the woman you have become." Ruby's smiling reflection answered yes. And Ruby nodded with approval.

Ruby decided to stay till her brother was fully recovered and walking around without help. Zach and Clara had a proper homecoming celebration with family, friends, and neighbors. Zola made some bite-size sandwiches in case visitors were hungry, and various neighbors dropped off casseroles for the rest of the week.

The next day Ruby popped in on her own to visit her brother. Clara and Zach were delighted to see her. After a while, he asked her why she had not gone back to Chicago yet.

"I wanted to be sure you were OK," Ruby said.

Zach shook his head. "After all the trouble you went through to become a working woman? And the hassle I went through to find you?" Clara swatted his head. "Well, it certainly panned out for me, didn't it?" He hugged his wife. "Now, Ruby, I don't want you wasting any more time here. Your boss won't wait forever, and there's no

doubt a man vying for your job while you're
away." He shooed her. "Now get back to
Chicago and make me proud."

Ruby gently hugged him, knowing his ribs
still hurt a bit.

"I can always count on you, Zach," said
Ruby. "I appreciate you understanding— and
looking after my friend."

She hugged Clara and planned to leave on
the next train to Chicago the following day.

She had mixed feelings about leaving but
knew she had to.

Zola hugged Ruby and told her she was very
proud of her but to not wait so long before
coming for another visit. Ruby promised and
gave her momma and extra squeeze goodbye.

Her dad drove her to the Drumright
station, parked the car, and told Ruby
he wanted to talk to her before she went
inside to catch her train. Ruby was a little
nervous, as her dad was not one to share his
emotions; she usually had to guess what he
was thinking.

"Ruby, it was great to have you here,
not just for Zach but for your momma," he
began. "She has missed you terribly; you will

never know how much till you have a child of your own." He paused and put his hands on her shoulders so she would look him in the eyes. "I am telling you this because I need you to write your momma more often; you have slacked off, and with so many of you grown up and all, she is just having a tough time adjusting to almost all of her children having their own lives. You know you have always been her favorite, and she has always admired your desire to tackle the world." He pulled her in for a hug, then released her. "So, do you think you could write her more?"

Ruby nodded and started to speak. He held his hand up to stop her.

"Let me finish and get this out," he said. "It is not easy for a dad to tell his friends he has a daughter that wants to be a working woman, much less that she lives in Chicago. Now I know I accepted that you were going and even drove you to the station and all, but to be honest, I thought you would find it so hard you would come back home and patch things up with Arthur." He chuckled. "But you surprised us all. You succeeded! Your momma and I are so proud of you. The world is changing, and I find myself bragging about you, and I want you to know it."

"Thank you, Dad, that means a lot," Ruby said.

"On the other hand, I know you realize your sisters, especially Rilla, are jealous of you. They would never admit it, but you have outgrown them. Heck, you have outgrown the whole town. I know you will never come back here to live, and I don't want you to. I only want you to come back to visit; though Tulsa would be a great place to live."

Ruby just looked at him, trying to think of something to say to lighten the mood. She even considered asking him about the John situation, since her dad had mentioned his "friends" but thought better of it. She wasn't angry anymore, and she was so touched by this moment with her dad and did not want to spoil it. He got out of the car, and Ruby hopped out and went to the other side where her dad was getting her suitcase to give him a big hug and kiss. He hugged her back and put some cash in her hands and they said their goodbyes. Ruby promised she would write more and come back home to visit more often.

Ruby thanked the Lord many times on the long train ride back to Chicago, and once back in her room at the Eleanor Club, she

immediately collapsed on her bed and slept
till it was time to go to work the next day.

∞ **218** ∞

Chapter 13

SURPRISE!

OCTOBER–NOVEMBER 1928

October had already arrived, and there was much to do at work between balancing the books and preparing for the holiday season just two months away. The cool weather was setting in again, and the Windy City was being true to its name.

Ruby had been working long hours, so she and Zoe decided it was time to relax. They called up Helen, who joined them, and they went to the Green Mill. They had had some great times there, so it was their go-to place. They had it down pat, and the doorman knew them, so there was no waiting in line. They walked right in and made their way to a booth, just far enough away from the band that they could enjoy drinks and still hear themselves talk.

Much to their surprise, and delight, The MacDougall Band was playing, and there was Mr. Clarinet Man. Zoe started teasing Ruby about him, and of course, Helen had to be filled in. This time Ruby made a point to watch him and was taken by the joy she could see in his face as he played.

Ruby did not dance this time, so there was no way he could have seen her, but he had recognized Zoe on the dance floor, and when the band took a break, he made his way over to their booth. The girls looked at Ruby when he came over and introduced himself. Zoe invited him to sit with them and have a drink, and he explained he did not drink but would enjoy a glass of water. So, there they sat making polite conversation, except this time he promised he would call.

Back at the Eleanor Club, before Ruby and Zoe parted for the night, Zoe said, "There is no doubt Clarinet Man will be contacting you. I see exciting times ahead for you." Ruby gave a half smile and shushed Zoe as they parted ways. Ruby entered her room and prepared for bed. She tried to sleep but was not ready, so she got out of bed and pulled out her journal.

The church service seemed to fly by, and
as always, Ruby enjoyed Minister John's
sermon. He always gave positive messages
and made her feel good about herself. Ruby's
church group was not meeting this Sunday,
so she took off for home, ready to relax and
have a quiet day.

Once home, she did her usual—kicked off

her shoes and changed into her robe, ready
to do nothing but read and prepare for the
week. It was to be a boring Sunday, which
was her favorite. Ruby made a sandwich,
poured a glass of milk, and sat in her
comfortable reading chair. She wanted to
finish the book she was reading, *The Hotel,*
which she had started just before her
world had turned upside down with Zach's
accident. She was looking forward to seeing
what would happen next.

Ruby was enjoying her sandwich as she
turned the pages of her book, and she was
getting caught up in the excitement of the
story when her phone rang. At the Eleanor
Club, each room had its own phone, which
made life much easier. Ruby could not
imagine who it could be. She knew all her
friends were busy. She picked up, and it was
none other than Edward. Ruby was surprised
he was calling so soon, and she was not
mentally prepared for it. They carried on
a polite conversation, and then finally, he
asked her if she would like to go to the
Lincoln Park Zoo with him and told her he
could pick her up.

Ruby looked down at what she was
wearing and was grateful he could not see
her at that moment. She hesitated.

"Oh, I must be disturbing you. Maybe on another day, then," he said quickly.

Ruby shook herself. "Oh no, not at all," she said. "I just was surprised to hear from you so soon. What time were you thinking?

"How about in an hour?"

"Sounds good. Last night you said you were familiar with the Eleanor Club, so I presume you know how to get here?"

"Oh, yes, I know where it is."
"So, just let the house mother know you are here for me, and she will ring me," said Ruby. "And I will come right down. See you at two!" She finished a bit breathless.

With that, Ruby quickly began to get ready, and of course, she had to call Zoe and tell her to come up and help her pick out the right dress to wear. She did not want to appear too casual or too overdressed. The girls had fun preparing Ruby, and before they knew it, the phone rang, and it was time for her to meet Edward. Zoe wished her good luck as Ruby made her way to the parlor where Edward was waiting.

They greeted each other then said goodbye to Mrs. Smith. When they walked out the front door, Ruby's eyes flew wide open when she saw Edward's car.

"Wow! What a car. I can't believe you have one of the latest!"

"Yup, isn't she a beauty? A 1928 Ford Model A Sport Coupe!" He brushed his hand over the hood. "I love cars, especially in my line of work."

"Oh, you mean as a musician?"

"That's what I do on the side. My full-time job is as a salesman for US Steel Corporation. We can talk more about it on our walk. I mentioned Lincoln Park. Does that still sound OK?"

"Fine, I like it there. It seems to be a favorite spot for afternoon walks. And it's so close to here."

"Well, I do enjoy it there, when I can get away. I sure am glad I have today to enjoy a walk with you."

Ruby smiled as they made their way to the zoo, where they saw a variety of animals and birds and chatted comfortably about each one.

"You were very smart to bring me here," she said, smiling at Edward. "It makes for easy conversation."

Edward smiled back at Ruby. "That's one way to look at it," he said. "But the other way is to think of it as an educational opportunity to learn more about the animals.

And, at the same time, we can get to know each other better. Animals have a way of drawing out a person's true nature."

Ruby raised her eyebrows and nodded in agreement.

They found a park bench close to the water where the swans were swimming. They sat and talked about whatever came to mind.

Edward shared why Lincoln Park was his favorite, not because of the size but its history. He shared with Ruby how it once was an old cemetery that was the burial place for many cholera victims, civil war rebels, and prisoners. Eventually, the cemetery was moved, mainly for health reasons.

"Now look at what a beautiful park it is! It goes to show that someone can have a wonderful vision, and with help, they can turn it into something beautiful for everyone to enjoy," he said. "I really love just sitting and listening to the birds sing to one another." He looked up into the trees and smiled.

Ruby loved that he was comfortable talking about such things.

"If you listen carefully, you can hear the notes for a new song or even the beginning of a symphony," he said.

Edward and Ruby listened quietly for a bit, then Edward hummed back what the birds sang. Ruby was fascinated by his love of nature and being inspired by the birds. She had never really thought of them like that. Ruby liked what he had said but felt there was a deeper meaning to the story, and maybe one day she would hear more. But for now, she was going to enjoy the company of a smart, sensitive man.

They continued exploring the zoo and enjoying the animals, and then they had a bite to eat from the hot dog vendor in the park. By the time they headed home, Ruby had made up her mind that she wanted to see him again. Thankfully, he did ask. So, they agreed to meet the following Saturday. Ruby was ready for a new adventure with Mr. Edward Rhodes.

Weeks went by, and Ruby and Edward became an item. Edward was in town more and was impressed with Ruby's understanding of how businesses ran, and they would discuss marketing ideas for when Edward approached potential clients to purchase steel from his company.

When they were not walking in the park or sharing a meal, Edward would join Ruby at her church and help with some of the humanitarian projects Ruby was working on. They talked about everything, from politics to family to books, and they even had debates on political issues. Ruby also shared with Edward how great her momma was in the kitchen and how she missed her cooking. She told him how much she loved her biscuits and gravy.

"Just wait till you have them, you won't want anyone else's biscuits," Ruby claimed.

Ruby shared with Zoe how Edward had not been to church in years but was happy to attend if it meant he would see her. She also told Zoe that when Edward came to pick her up from work, and she would see him waiting for her inside the store, her heart would jump. He had a way of just making her heart flutter. Zoe was excited for Ruby to have finally found someone.

"Now don't be getting ahead of yourself," Ruby told Zoe. "It is still early days with us seeing one another."

Zoe raised an eyebrow at Ruby.

"OK, I am hopeful," Ruby admitted with a grin.

One evening over dinner, Ruby told Edward she wanted to know more about his childhood. She wondered why he hadn't told her anything at all about it. He looked at her with sad eyes, as he had before when she had brought up his childhood.

"It's difficult to discuss," he said.

Ruby took his hand. "If we want to build a relationship, then I must know you, and you must know me."

He patted her hand. "Ruby, you have truly stolen my heart. I will open up to you but not here." He sat back. "Let's enjoy our meal, and then we'll find a place to sit and talk."

Ruby agreed, and they finished their meal and chatted about work, politics, and various things happening in other parts of the world. Ruby and Edward could talk about anything and were basically always on the same page. If they disagreed, they would just have a discussion; if there was no agreement, they would call it a draw so that they would not ruin the night. It turned out both of them enjoyed a friendly debate. It was a way to find out how a person thought and who they were at their very core.

After dinner, they walked to the car, and
Edward opened the door, as it was polite to
do so, but it was also a way to give Ruby a
quick peck on the check. Once Edward was in
the driver's seat, he didn't start the car.

"Is everything all right?" she asked.

"I am trying to think of a place to go. Let
me think for a moment." Ruby sat quietly, as
she recognized *that* voice. Edward sounded
like one of her brothers trying to figure
something out.

After a few minutes, Edward looked at
her. "Is it too chilly for you to sit outside by
the fountain and talk?"

"I'm happy to do that," she said. "I'm
bundled up enough."

Edward nodded, started the car up, and
headed to the park. Once they arrived, he
got out, went around, and opened the door
for her. The two walked hand in hand over to
the fountain. Lucky for them, a couple had
just left the bench in front of the fountain,
so they sat down where the other couple had
already warmed the seat.

Ruby gave Edward a soft smile, and he
looked at her and then looked away. Ruby
could sense he was not ready to talk, so
she kept quiet, hoping he would begin to feel

comfortable about opening up. It seemed like an eternity.

Finally, Edward began talking. "If I'm going to get through this, you absolutely cannot interrupt me." He looked at Ruby, and she nodded. "No questions either. I just want to get it out. I have never spoken to anyone about my childhood till now."

Ruby smiled and patted his hand.

"Ruby, if continuing to see you means I have to reveal more of myself, then I will do it."

Later, Ruby filled Zoe in on the whole story. Her heart had broken as she and Zach sat there, and she had wanted so much to ask questions and make remarks, but she had held her tongue. The sadness in his eyes had revealed the pain he carried from those days.

"When he was finished, he asked me not to comment," Ruby said. "And we just walked back to the car, and he took me home. We parted, and he said he would call. Edward could not even look me in the eyes. The next thing I know, I am knocking at your door, wanting to talk to someone."

"Of course, I'm always here for you."

Zoe hugged her. "Can I ask . . . what was so horrible?"

"I'm not ready to discuss it, and I'm not even sure if I should. It is not as bad as it sounds but still something that would hurt any child."

Ruby thanked Zoe for listening. Even though she hadn't shared the full details, she still felt better, and went to her place.

Every night after work, Ruby looked to see if a message had been left for her at the front desk, but nothing. Ruby thought it was so weird she hadn't heard from Edward. He had done the hardest part, now the rest should be easy. Two weeks passed and not a word. Another two weeks passed, and Thanksgiving was coming.

Finally, Ruby came home to a letter. She could not wait to get to her room and read it.

Dear Ruby,

Sorry to have been so quiet. I appreciate you just listening while I shared my past. I had hoped to see

*you sooner, but work went crazy. I
know what you are thinking, but truly
my work has been very hectic. I was
sent to Pittsburgh to work in the
office there for a month and a half.
It is hard to believe it is going to be
Thanksgiving soon. I am going to go to
Iowa to see my dad, and hopefully all
is well.*

*I should be back in town in
December, and I want to be sure we
see one another. I will contact you as
soon as I get to town.*

*Love,
Edward*

Ruby quietly folded the letter and put
it away, muttering to herself, wondering if
she had done the right thing by prying into
his past. It had seemed painful for him,
but he had decided it was fine because he
wanted to continue to be with her and build
her trust.

Ruby put her head down and focused on
work. She watched as more people were
laid off and the world continued to spiral.
With Thanksgiving coming, Ruby thought of
the lovely Thanksgivings she had had while

in college, but mostly she recalled how things seemed much simpler back then. Ruby wondered why she had been in such a hurry to grow up.

The rest of November seemed to fly by, and life felt monotonous. Work, work, work, bosses being worried about unsold inventory, more people being laid off. The merriment of the early '20s had passed, and life was no longer easy.

Reports in the news always highlighted the industrial age advantages, but the downside was job losses. Politicians encouraged people to learn a new skill, but that was easier said than done.

The accounting department at Ruby's company reported that they still had too much merchandise, but putting it all on sale would be risky. It would be hard to go back to regular prices, as people might wait for the next sale, which would lead to the company taking big losses.

Ruby shared with Zoe one evening that the top accountants were trying to convince the buyers at work to purchase fewer products and that it wasn't the right time to be expanding the store's product line, but it was taking some convincing. It seemed that most of the buyers believed that buying only what you could afford was old-fashioned. Offering credit to customers allowed them to enjoy new products like electric washing machines, living room sets, diamond rings, and dresses made of silk instead of cotton. The buyers wanted The Fair to keep up with the times.

"What does it matter?" Zoe asked.

Ruby was amazed at her response. "Well, there is a negative to every positive. Fewer cotton products mean less cotton to be grown on the farm. Electric washing machines mean the person hired to wash clothes has less income," she explained. "There is a reactive effect, and we see it clearly when looking at the books. If people don't have money to spend, stores have fewer products, and those people relying on credit and not saving for a rainy day could be in trouble. Plus, have you not heard about the work lines forming because of men being replaced by machinery?"

Ruby was on a roll and wanted to keep going, but Zoe did not want to hear any more.

"Ruby, I just want the good times to keep rolling. This conversation is too depressing."

Ruby sighed. "I forgot you don't like debates. I was hoping you would have some thoughts to counter what I am saying."

"No, I don't. And I want more coffee . . . preferably made by the fancy coffee machine you have," Zoe said with a giggle.

Ruby said, "Touché," and changed the topic.

They enjoyed their coffee and listened to some of their favorite songs, like "Singin' the Blues" by Frankie Trumbauer and his Orchestra with Bix Beiderbecke, before calling it a night.

One Friday night, Ruby received a phone call from her momma, responding to a letter Ruby had written asking for some motherly advice. Ruby had shared with her momma how she thought Edward was the one and how his childhood was so sad. Ruby was pleasantly surprised to hear her momma's voice since it was not even Sunday, when it was less expensive to call. Zola told Ruby not to worry about the cost of the call. She had read her letter and wanted to respond,

and Ruby's dad had agreed that the sooner
the better.

Right off the bat, Zola asked, "Do you
love this Edward? You know we have not
even met him."

Ruby explained how she had mixed feelings
but felt it could be more and just wanted
her momma to know what was going on. Zola
was a good listener but always gave her two
cents' worth, especially when it came to
her children.

"You know, Ruby, your dad and I never
understood your need to be part of a man's
world," she said. "But we do understand how
the world has changed, and even the concept
of dating is so different from our day. These
days a man and woman can just go out for
a fun evening on the town." She sighed. "Of
course, we want you to marry, but you have
not really courted—or, excuse me, dated—
enough to know if he is really the best match
for you."

Ruby tried to interject, but her momma
insisted she say what she had called to say
without Ruby interrupting.

Ruby agreed to listen.

"Now, Ruby, there are all kinds of love,
and there is nothing more special than that
first person you feel love toward, but that

does not necessarily mean you marry them. Marriage is more than just a passion for one another. Passion wears off, and the living together begins. Of course, you still want to be attracted to the person, but it is when the day-to-day grind of daily life comes about that you realize marriage is also a business. Now, ask yourself whether he can afford it. I mean, when you start a family, and you need to be home to nurse the baby, can he still support you?

"Money is not everything, but it helps. Now the other thing I wanted to say is, and remember you asked for my thoughts, Edward comes from a broken home; his mother ran away and left him with his dad. If I read your letter correctly, to sum it up, his dad remarried, Edward's stepmother kicked him out of the house, and his two grandmothers raised him. So, Ruby, you are right, and I can see why you feel he needs rescuing. Well, it is not your place to save him. Now, I have not met him, but I am here to tell you some people do not need to be rescued. So, you think long and hard." She paused. "OK, now you can talk."

"Wow, Momma, I did not expect all of this," Ruby said. "I do appreciate all you have said and will think long and hard about it. I do feel sorry for Edward, and, having lived on my own and experienced the world, I have discovered how lucky I am to have you and Dad for parents. Oilton was a great place to grow up. I have always felt loved by my whole family and even the community. I never knew people could be unloved. I had never heard of a mom walking out on her family. I find it tragic." Ruby paused and collected her thoughts. "Momma, I am not saying I am going to marry him. He has not asked me, and I don't even know if he loves me. I wrote you because I know I am a late bloomer compared to my sisters in this type of situation. I just wanted to share, and I know if I were home, you would be asking me what is on my mind. I was missing you, so I thought I would write you."

"Well, sweetie, remember what I have always told you to think about when making your choices—things can change in the blink of an eye. Think about the different paths based on a decision. I won't tell you what to do, as it is your life. But I will always be here to support you in whatever decision you make."

"Thank you, Momma."

"Now, you are correct—early love blossoming is very special, and I'm happy someone makes you smile. However, I chuckled when I heard you made him a pie. That is when I knew I should call. I don't recall you telling me you made a pie for any man before." They both laughed. "Well, unless you have any other questions, I better hang up. Everybody is good here. We love you, Ruby."

"Love you too, Momma." With that, Ruby hung up and grinned. *Just like Momma to call and give me more to think about.*

Ruby sat down and started to make a list of Edward's qualities that she liked, but then ripped up the paper. *For once, I am not going to be so practical. I am just going to live.* She threw away the shreds of paper and got ready for bed.

Chapter 14

DECISION TIME

DECEMBER 1928—JANUARY 1, 1929

Ruby was leaving work to catch the streetcar home on a cold December morning when a huge grin appeared on her face. There was Edward at the front door, waiting for her. Of course, Ruby was thrilled to see him. It seemed like an eternity since they had seen one another. They had so much to catch up on. Edward invited her to dinner, and she accepted without hesitation.

Edward explained all about the steel companies in Pittsburgh and the opportunities ahead. He would be spending more time in Pittsburgh, but Ruby was happy to hear that he would be called to fill in at the home office every so often.

He assured Ruby that nothing would change between them and that he would be faithful even when he was away. He told her he loved her and knew his luck had changed the moment he met her.

Ruby smiled, happy to have finally heard those three little words. She was content, for the time being, with Edward's plans. Life seemed to proceed as usual with everyone preparing for Christmas. The accounting department was busy preparing for the closing of the books and the January audit. Edward was called away once more. However, Ruby did not mind Edward being gone, as she enjoyed her independence and her ability to continue to grow in her own work.

All of Ruby's friends were moving on with their lives, getting married, and having babies, while Ruby stayed constant with her work and even moved up with a promotion in the accounting department. It could not have been better.

As Christmas approached, Ruby heard from home; it seemed like everyone in her family was moving forward as well. It was hard to believe that Ida Jane was married. Most of her brothers were family men now, and her dad still had his hand in politics in Oilton and Drumright.

Her momma had won several state cooking awards for her watermelon pickles and her pickled cucumbers. She even found time to sew for others in the community, and she was enjoying that immensely.

It was Christmas Eve when Ruby received a call that she had a visitor downstairs. She could not imagine who it was, as Edward was not in town. She quickly got dressed and made herself presentable in case it was her boss. Lo and behold, it was Edward. He had arrived in town early. Ruby was so excited to see him. She wanted to hug him but resisted, as she did not want to be considered a hussy.

They left the building, and Edward took her to a quiet diner to tell her what was going on.

Much to her surprise, Edward started talking about a new job he was taking in Pittsburgh, still in the steel business. He explained all the great reasons to go with the new company and what it meant for his future.

"Ruby, none of this will mean anything unless you are part of my future," he said as he reached into the pocket of his tailored blue suit, pulled out a box, and popped the question. "Ruby, will you marry me?"

Ruby was tongue-tied. The engagement ring was a single large diamond on a silver band. Misunderstanding her silence, Edward told her she could exchange it for a different ring if she wished. Ruby looked at him, still tongue-tied.

"Ruby, I know how much you love being independent. I would never take that away from you." He held her hand. "You can find a job in Pittsburgh, and we can hire a housekeeper and a cook so that you would not have to do anything but relax when you came home in the evenings. We can relax together and talk about our days."

He went on to tell her how he admired her and would be proud to have a modern woman for his wife if she agreed to marry him.

Ruby looked into his big brown eyes and was ready to say no as she quieted him with her finger touching his lips.

"How soon do you have to return to Pittsburgh?" she asked.

"January 15, so I was thinking, if you said yes, we could elope." His enthusiasm started to build. "We could have a small honeymoon and then begin preparing for the move. The company knows all about you and has agreed if we are man and wife, they will pack and move your things as well as mine. What do you say?"

Ruby was ready to say no and stay the course, but before she knew it, her heart spoke up, and she uttered, "Yes!" One she realized what she had said, she knew her heart was right. Ruby saw Edward's eyes fill with joy. She was over the moon to have finally met a modern man who believed women could work outside of the house. She was a lucky girl. She *could* have it all!

Ruby gave a one-week notice at work, and she and Edward eloped on New Year's Day. Her friends were very surprised but ecstatic. Everything seemed to fall into place. Ruby was now twenty-five, and by society's standards, she was an old maid and lucky that someone would even have her. But in Ruby's eyes, she had worked toward a dream and gotten an education, she was a modern working woman, and she was now ready to embrace sharing her life with Edward.

When Ruby and Edward stepped off the train
in Pittsburgh, she smiled at him. She threw
back her shoulders and looked around.

"Well, Pittsburgh, get ready. Ruby Pearl
has arrived!"

ABOUT THE AUTHOR

Diann Floyd Boehm is an award-winning, international author, community volunteer, humanitarian, and former classroom teacher. She is passionate about storytelling and has published many picture books for children and two young adult historical novels. In addition, Diann is a co-host for several shows on **USA Global TV**. Diann is married, a mother of three, and has one grandchild. Diann loves to inspire readers of all ages to "Embrace Imagination!" You can learn more about the author and her books at ocpublishing.ca/diann-floyd-boehm.html or diannfloydboehm.com.

*Other books by Diann Floyd Boehm,
published by OC Publishing:*

Rise! A Girl's Struggle for More

Charlie and the Tire Swing

Moonling Adventures — The Serengeti

Harry the Camel (English and
   Arabic versions)

The Little Girl in the Moon

The Little Girl in the Moon — The Big Idea

The Little Girl in the Moon — Moxie &
   Tycho Town